Earth: Elemental Reverse Harem Quartet

Elemental Reverse Harem Quartet, Volume 1

Helen J Perry

Published by H J Perry, 2019.

This edition revised and reedited March 2023

Cover by ReddHott Covers
Editing by Pair of Nines

This book contains sexually explicit content which is suitable only for mature readers.

Written in British English with mostly American spelling.

Author's website: HelenJPerry.com

CHAPTER ONE

N*othing like a hound dog in London*
Malka Selby

GLOBULES OF SALIVA dripped from menacing canine teeth. The enormous black dogs looked hungry, violent, and much too close for comfort. Heaven knows how I didn't see them approaching before they came within five feet.

When I noticed them, it was too late. The dog duo rushed forward, tugging at the ends of their very long leashes, and their warm breaths smelled of raw meat, death, and decay.

I only had an instant to register my distaste before a sudden gust of wind knocked me off balance. It forced me to step back, to steady myself. The same blast of air brought the dogs to a temporary halt as if a solid but invisible wall forced its way between us. As a bonus, it blew the stench of their poor oral hygiene in another direction.

The reprieve lasted only a moment before the dogs lunged. It all happened so fast that I didn't see the dogs' owner.

My life flashed in front of my eyes, but I never discovered how it ended.

A man stepped between the slathering hounds and me, and not a moment too soon. His rapid hand movements blurred in front of him while I froze, helpless with terror.

The creatures slowly slinked backward. They appeared as stunned as I was, and that was when I saw each of them had their massive, powerful jaws wrapped around what you might call a stick. It appeared more like two giant dogs the size of horses chewing on baby tree trunks.

The man whose intervention had cut short my terrifying ordeal altered the course of my first twenty-four hours in London.

"Are you all right?" When he turned to face me, he looked about my age, early twenties. I expected heroes to be older. Like his clothes and his tightly curled hair, his eyes were almost completed black, a mostly dilated pupil surrounded by a slither of the darkest brown I'd ever seen.

"I'm fine," I lied; I was shaken. "No harm done to me, but what about you? What were you thinking? Did you see the size of those teeth? They might have eaten you whole." I talk a lot when I'm shaken. "They weren't normal. Do you usually step into danger like that? And why were you carrying those logs?"

As if I was a wild animal in need of soothing, he raised his hand, palm towards me. "I saw the dogs from some distance away and noticed that you hadn't seen them. I simply picked up the first things I saw lying on the street to use for defense." His hands swept the space in front of him as he answered calmly. He didn't appear shaken at all. Anyone would think battling rabid dogs was all part of an ordinary night out in London.

"Thank you." Glancing over his shoulder, I expected to see the dogs and their owners, but they'd vanished, possibly taking a turn down a side street.

A second figure appeared alongside my savior, but I paid him no attention until he asked, "Do you need any help?"

Still trembling with fear and shock, I shook my head. "No, thanks. I'm fine." *Not fine at all.*

"We can escort you to the station or stay with you if you're waiting for a lift, if you want." Apparently, these two men were together. "Don't worry; we'll make sure you don't see those hell hounds again."

Hell hounds? Is that the official name of the breed?

A fitting name. I'd never seen anything like them.

"I'm sure I'll be fine," I repeated like the part of my brain that controlled speech was stuck in one groove. There were no dogs within sight, so I readjusted my eyes to focus on the gallant men.

Two sets of concerned eyes watched me. I had the full attention of two handsome young men, so the night wasn't all bad.

"Really, I'll be okay. I'm staying in this hotel right here." I nodded at the building to my left. We stood just a few feet from the door. "I don't need to go anywhere. It was just bad timing that I met those dogs. A minute later, and I'd have been safely inside."

At least chatting distracted me from dwelling on the lucky escape. And these men weren't just any listeners but two distractingly hot guys. I refocused again to make sure they really were young, handsome, and gallant. To my mind, those things didn't go together in the twenty-first century, did they?

"We're staying in this same hotel." My savior tilted his head and raised his dark eyebrows in surprise. An attractive smile formed on his appealing full lips. "Let's get inside, shall we?"

I liked the way his tongue licked his lips after he spoke. I wouldn't mind hearing him saying the same thing to me *(let's get inside, shall we?)* under very different circumstances that also involved licking.

Chivalrously, he rolled his arm and bent his body in a slight bow as he said, "After you."

Another freakish gust of wind blew along the street. I shivered and moved toward the door, fishing my keycard from my pocket at the same time. It was just after midnight, so the outer door was locked, or at least it should have been.

A group of people on their way out of the hotel held the door open for the three of us, making the white square of plastic redundant. The polite action by these strangers made me wonder how easily people who weren't guests could just wander into the hotel. It didn't bear thinking about. And then I stopped thinking about that because the elevator was waiting for us with the doors open.

"We're on the third floor. You're welcome to come to our room for a drink if you want some company while you get over the shock." The sultry voice of the other guy issued the invitation as we entered the small square box. His warm breath caressed my ear.

"But I don't know you." I hit the button for the third floor.

My erogenous areas tingled with arousal.

My brain should have sent me danger alerts about entering a hotel room outnumbered by two strange men. Instead, it occurred to me that being ravished in a hotel room by wild boys was far preferable to being savaged by wild dogs.

"My name's Charlie," said the dark handsome savior with the fast hands. And broad shoulders. And intense dark eyes. "And this is Neal."

"Now you know our names, and we have beer," Neal added, like they were a double act.

"I'm Malka, and I like the sound of a beer. I mean, I like the taste of it too. If you want to talk about beer drinking, I'm all for it."

Leaning against the wall of the elevator with his thumbs hooked in the top of his low hanging jeans, Charlie flashed a seductive smile. "Well, Malka who likes beer, that's put us all on first-name terms. Just say if there's anything else we can do to make you happy." He carried on grinning: all milky white teeth contrasting with his warm acorn skin.

Undress?

My brain flooded with inappropriate ideas before I thought of an answer that I could share.

"You should send a message to a friend telling her where you are. That's a way to make sure you're safe." Neal's suggestion endeared him to me. I'd gotten the measure of him already. A thoughtful and kind man with a smoldering, sexy friend.

I didn't have a phone and couldn't text anyone, but it wasn't something I'd often admit to. I didn't want people to think of me as pathetic or a freak. The fact was, I was the only adult on the planet without a mobile phone. I'd acknowledge the weirdness of my situation only to my closest friends. Me and technology, we didn't get along. Maybe I should have been born at least a century earlier. And in the current situation, I could do without the strangers believing I was vulnerable.

Shrugging in what I intended as a carefree way, I said, "I'm on the third floor as well, so it wouldn't be too far out of my way to stop by for a sociable drink with you guys. And my instincts tell me you're good people."

We arrived on the third floor. Charlie led the way, and I followed his swagger along the corridor to their room.

"Malka—it's an unusual name." Neal walked beside me. He must have noticed that I had fixed my gaze on his friend's arse, but he didn't comment on that.

"I guess it might be. I've met a few women with the same name while I've been traveling, but none in England. The name's Jewish and means queen."

"Are you a Jewish queen?"

I laughed. "I wasn't raised as any religion. I'm not sure about my ancestors. I expect they were Christian, as most English people are. And I went to a Christian school." And I hoped we'd leave my background there. I didn't like confessing to either a privileged education in an elite private school afforded by only the richest families, along with the fact of my criminally absent parents. It was all too out of the ordinary.

"Sounds much the same as us." Charlie swiped the plastic keycard. It didn't work. He tried it again and then again. The third time brought success, and he switched on the light as he led the way into the room. He sat down on one of the two beds and pointed to the only chair for me.

These dudes were easy to get along with, and as we were all staying in a budget hotel at King's Cross, we had plenty in common, for sure. They were British, judging by their accents, and about my age.

At least they had two beds, which was lucky for them.

Betty and I had to share a bed. We'd only pitched up at the hotel a few hours earlier, searching for a room when we arrived straight off the train in from mainland Europe. It was dusk, and the hotel only had a few rooms left. We had no choice but to take a room for two sleeping in the same bed. Still, Betty was my dear friend from school, and we'd just spent years traveling and roughing it together. This wasn't the first time we'd shared a bed.

"Beer? Or something stronger?" Neal offered. He'd trailed in behind and remained near the door to rummage through their luggage. He held up a bottle and a bottle opener. "We're prepared for most things, so long as it requires alcohol."

From where I sat, I had a good opportunity to watch him. Neal was just as fit as his friend. Appearance-wise, they looked like a couple of magazine fashion models. The sort of guys who would have no trouble tempting different women back to their rooms every night. Yet, I'd found them making their way back to their hotel room empty-handed, or they would have been if they hadn't met me outside. And they didn't seem arrogant, which I associated with guys who looked like that.

After kicking his shoes off, Charlie lay back, stretching out on the bed. "Or, if you prefer, not so strong? We've got bottles of water."

A pack of nine sat on the desk beside me, unopened and still wrapped in aqua-blue plastic. I couldn't miss them.

"I'll go for a beer, thanks. It's after midnight. Don't you think it's rather late for people to be out walking their dogs?"

"Dunno." Charlie placed his hands behind his head, which was only slightly raised by his pillow. His T-shirt rode up, revealing washboard abs. "I've never had a dog."

In time to rehydrate my drying mouth, Neal handed me a bottle of lager and a bottle opener. I levered the metal top loose from the bottle and gave the opener back. Taking a big glug from the bottle, I downed half of it in no time. "If those dogs got closer without biting, I'd have died from dog-breath intoxication. They should've been wearing muzzles. What breed did you say they were? Do you think they're on the dangerous dog breeds register?"

"I've no idea. They were too big to be pit bulls." Neal perched on the very edge of his bed with his knees wide apart and two beers in his hands, one apparently for Charlie.

"Didn't one of you mention a dog breed before?" I asked. I thought they'd called the dogs by a specific name, but the word had fallen from my memory. They exchanged glances and didn't answer.

"You know, while we were away, we spent many a night telling stories around campfires on beaches." Neal shifted his weight on the bed. "I'm not suggesting we light a fire in this room, but we'd be more comfortable if we put the pillows and duvets on the floor. It'd be cozy."

Charlie swung his legs around to place his feet back on the floor. "Great idea, Na—, Neal. more comfortable and closer." He stood up and threw his bedding into the pit between the beds.

"I'm all for it," I agreed. Anything to get off the plastic chair that was designed to be cheap and robust rather than stylish and comfortable. Dropping down next to Charlie, I made myself at home on his bed linen pile, which involved sitting right up close to him. I was aware of the warmth of his arm next to mine and the faint pleasant scent of cologne.

Before joining us in the makeshift pit of cushions, Neal got up and gathered more drinks, both beer and water. He put them on the floor at the foot of his bed. "We might need sustenance within arm's reach." Not only was he a practically minded and attentive gentleman, I decided he was every bit as sexy as his friend.

Charlie leaned forward to accept a beer bottle opened by Neal. "I like the way you're thinking. Cheers, mate."

When he sat down opposite me, Neal stretched his long legs out beside me, on the other side from Charlie. Neal picked up my feet and removed my shoes, putting them to one side. He placed my feet, still in their socks, onto his lap.

Attempting to control my emotions, I focused on what had brought me to their room. "Wouldn't it be unfortunate to be killed by a dog just a few feet from the safety of my hotel?"

Neal's fingers pressed firmly against the bases of both feet as he rubbed them. "You were never in any danger."

How do you know that?

I merely purred as his fingers began to work the soles of my feet. Instead of telling him how much I liked what he was doing, I said, "Says the man who stood by and watched but did nothing." Intended as friendly banter, my teasing may have sounded harsh. "Hey, don't worry. I wouldn't have saved you from a rabid brutal beast, either. The man who stepped in front of those dogs needs a sanity check." I nudged Charlie in the ribs and realized we were actually leaning on one another. "If your friend wasn't there, I think they'd have had my throat."

"You do know hardly anyone dies from dog bites? Especially not in England. The dogs were more than likely going to lick you all over before I gave them those sticks to chew on." Charlie picked up a bottle of water and pushed it into my hands. "Water before more beer."

I couldn't disagree with that wisdom.

Neal passed me my second bottle of the amber nectar, again lid still sealed firmly in place. After all the bad stories I'd heard on my travels of drinks being spiked, I appreciated seeing sealed bottles. I felt safe with these guys.

"If there's any dog who'd want to lick you all over, it's my mate sitting beside you," Neal said.

"Fuck off, Neal. I'm not a dog."

My heart beat a little faster. I ignored Charlie's rebuff and asked Neal, "He's good with his tongue, is he?"

Neal flashed a cheeky grin. His eyes sparkled. "If there was going to be any nuzzling involved, I think it's Ch—, Charlie, who's your man for the job."

As Neal stuttered, the temperature in the room rose a couple of degrees. A warm breeze circled my neck; I thought the hotel room air conditioning must have clicked on.

Neal might have tapped into my horny brainwaves with his comment, but I could raise the ante.

"Only Charlie? My friend Betty's gone off to spend the night with two guys she met this evening." Lucky Betty. "I don't think one of the guys was going to be left out. In fact, isn't there a saying, *'one man's good and two men are better'*?"

Charlie turned his head towards me, which put his mouth very near mine. "I'm not impressed by a friend leaving you alone in London like that, where you might be attacked and eaten by wild beasts."

"You just said hardly anyone ever dies because of a dog bite, as if I was at more risk of being run over by the night bus." My body might react in the usual way to how gorgeous this man looked and smelled, but the feminist in me refused to let any man tell me women need to take additional precautions for our own safety simply because we were women. Even if I had enjoyed him being gallant and chivalrous. "Anyway, she didn't just abandon me. She asked me if it was okay. We were only in the bar next to the hotel. A girl should be able to walk from one building to another, just a few yards, at any time of day or night."

Having reached the ends of my feet, Neal squeezed my toes. "I agree with you. The streets should be safe for everyone. I'm not so sure about your misquote. Isn't it from Orwell's Animal Farm? We read it in school."

His fingers distracted me by kneading my heel and ankle, and I wondered what else those strong fingers could do. I had no idea that feet in general, and my toes in particular, had a direct connection with the clitoris.

"I read Animal Farm at my school too." Even I heard how breathless I sounded when I spoke. And it wasn't George Orwell that had me gasping.

"Then you remember it wrong. It's *four legs good, two legs better.*" Charlie's voice sounded like a low-pitched purring lion in my ear.

My insides heated to the core, and one area became considerably wetter.

"Hmm, that can't be right." I pointed at Charlie. "You've got two legs, and he's got two legs. Four's definitely better. You two saved me from the jaws of death, and I think I'm entitled to celebrate the splendid things being alive has to offer." I turned my face toward Charlie. His face was right there next to mine. His rough-stubbled cheek scratched against me, but when it met mine, his mouth was something else. He tasted of red-hot, sexy man: yes, that is an official flavor.

Even though I was busy kissing his friend, Neal didn't stop working on my feet. He pulled my toes and twisted his fingers around and in between them and twisting the cotton sock fabric at the same time. He squeezed my little toe and said, "This little piggy went to market." Moving to the next toe, he did the same. "This little piggy went to school." And then the next. As he worked through the digits, each squeeze and pull tugged away a layer of my protective inhibitions and took away my breath.

"This little piggy had none." Neal's voice sounded sultry.

Pulling away from Charlie, I declared, "There's no need for any of us to have none." And I resumed the kiss while they took me closer to squealing all the way home.

Although this seemed sluttish and forward of me, I'd never felt safer. It was like I'd known these guys forever. And, what's more, I'd grown sick of being careful and boring. I'd done that for years while traveling in countries where I didn't speak the national language. I'd come back without a personal horror story about being raped or drugged, thank goodness, but I'd not slept with nearly enough people, in my opinion, and I'd never had a threesome.

Neal didn't disappoint when his little piggy ran home. Firmly, he stroked his hand right up my leg and up the inside of my thigh. The movement was slow enough for me to call a halt if I'd wanted to (I didn't), but fast enough to be perfect.

Don't stop.

"Don't stop."

CHAPTER TWO

Gasping for air in the King's Cross hotel
Malka Selby

SLOWLY, I SLIPPED BACKWARD until I lay on the makeshift mattress of duvet and pillows between the beds. Charlie came with me, his lips sealed with mine in a breathtaking kiss that continued when he was half on top of me.

A warm breeze seemed to whip around the room; it must have come in through an open window, even though the sound of traffic did not. Or it might have been a silent air conditioning system, if such a thing existed.

Neal moved with me too. He changed his position so that he lay next to me. Meanwhile, his hand smoothed up and over my jeans, pausing when he reached the sensitive part at the top of my inner thigh. Thick denim didn't prevent this from feeling incredible and intimate. His warm hand cupped my crotch. The pressure of his fingers created friction where it mattered most and where I wanted them. He pressed against my nub. He didn't stop there. His hand continued up, and he popped the top button of my jeans but attempted to disrobe me no further.

I gasped when he tucked his fingers just under the waistband of my jeans and stroked my bare stomach. Instead of going deeper, he drew his hand up under my top until he found Charlie's hand already cupping one of my breasts. Luckily, I have two.

Neal's hand worked its way under Charlie's body until I had the hands of two men squeezing my breasts and teasing my nipples.

I broke my kiss with Charlie to turn and kiss Neal. And why not? Neither of the men seemed to mind sharing me, so I intended to make the most of it.

I hadn't figured out where to put my own hands, so I decided using them to pop open my jeans and push them down might be an excellent move. It was already late at night, and I wanted to encourage these guys to get on with things, not politely take their time. I didn't need seducing.

When Charlie realized what I was doing, he sat up. I was too busy with my mouth attached to the other guy's face to check on Charlie, but he batted my hands away and took over. He pulled my jeans and underwear right down my legs and all the way off.

Bare arousal swept through me. Some of it seeped out on to Charlie's fingers as they slipped over my moist folds. "You're so very wet." His low breathy voice sounded in awe of my wetness, but the two of them had only themselves to blame. And if he thought that was wet, I ought to warn him about the coming flood.

There was no way the dam of self-control would stay in place for long. Not when my hands were exploring the undulating landscape of Neal's sculpted torso and while his hand taunted my bullet-hard nipple. He turned out to have the physique of a god under his clothes. His kisses tasted of pure sex.

An orgasm very soon was almost guaranteed.

Especially as long as a second, equally sexy guy touched me *there.*

Please, don't stop.

Although I'd have liked more attention inside me as well, Charlie didn't keep stroking me.

It was too much for my sanity. Didn't he hear me say, *don't stop*? The bastard would make me beg. Before I pushed Neal away so that I could beg, Charlie shoved my legs apart.

Jeez.

He slipped his broad shoulders between my knees. My private lady-parts became available for his scrutiny, and looking wasn't all he'd do.

Oh, mercy.

His hot tongue was just what I wanted right then, and exactly what I got.

Fuck me.

Squirming under his touch, I didn't want to throw him off, but the sensations his mouth delivered to my clit weren't the sort of thing a woman could stay still for.

I bent my knees and planted my feet firmly on the floor so I could raise my pelvis up toward the source of pleasure. And I held on to Neal as if my life depended on it, kissing him for all he was worth.

Kissing and moaning into his mouth and thrusting upwards. My juices flowed like he'd tapped into a buried water source and my love tunnel had sprung a leak. My body was doing its own thing, no longer under my conscious control. My brain worked in its own mysterious way, too.

I was going to fucking come right there and then like that between these two guys, who still had all their clothes on and didn't seem to mind if I used them for my sexual gratification.

Fuck me. Fingers.

I was too aroused for one finger, and I wasn't sure I'd have felt it in my channel, which was awash with more lubricant than many well-oiled machines.

Fortunately, he pushed far more than one finger inside. I didn't see, but I'd guess three. And just like that, my body contorted, cramped, spasmed, and urged him to thrust in and out.

He did. *Good boy.* He thrust in and out with his fingers and kept his mouth over my clit, and I tried not to thrash about—not too much—through my orgasm.

The air was sucked from my lungs.

I was breathless.

Gasping for oxygen.

Climactic sensations seized me.

Not only did I come, but I let myself go—true and complete release. In a way that I never dreamed possible with men I'd only just met. With strangers.

I relaxed in a way that was usually only possible on my own. I hoped I'd one day find myself at such uninhibited ease with a lover. Someone I knew well and trusted. It seemed impossible—this level of arousal, of carefree abandon... with strangers. And yet I was there. Living it.

When I came, the men didn't stop and withdraw from me, like other lovers I'd had.

Charlie slowed his movements right down, and a finger dropped from my pussy, but he didn't pull out completely. He didn't remove his tongue from my clit either, not until I pushed him away.

Charlie licked around his lips before wiping his face on the back of his hand. "You taste magical. I could never get enough of you."

Neal huffed. "I wish I were in his position, but your mouth tastes amazing, too. I've wanted to kiss you since forever."

"We've only just met." I ran my hand down to grope the bulge of his crotch. Neal's dick was hard, thick, and long, and I wanted it.

"Have we?" He groaned. "It seems as if I've known you forever."

He wanted something.

I moved to undo his jeans, but his hand fell over mine. "Hold on. I'm already on the edge."

"What about you, Charlie? Are you all right down there?" I looked down my body at the other man, who grinned back at me, looking very pleased with himself.

He gave me a thumbs-up sign with one hand. The other was still attached to my do-da. "Hope you're ready for more."

"Are you kidding? This is my first ever threesome. I don't mind if it goes on all night." *So I've got a great story to tell Betty*, I thought, but

I didn't tell them that bit. "But I shouldn't be the only person without pants."

Two grinning guys shook off their clothes, tops and bottoms. I still wore my top, but I did not attempt to remove it. For one thing, it was a bit breezy in their room, although it had stayed warm enough. And for another, watching the two men strip commanded all my attention.

They had the bodies of supermodels. It was a little intimidating, and I thought I might never get to shag anyone so easy on the eye ever again, so I'd better make the most of it.

And then there was the bonus of two men at once.

"If you enjoyed what we just did, I'd like to swap positions and have a turn at eating your pussy."

Oh, god. Yes.

I expected they'd want to get on with the fucking, eventually. Possibly double-entry or spit roast. Wasn't that what men wanted when they shared a girl? And I wasn't about to say no. I wanted to try those things too, but I'd be more than willing for more pussy-licking and kissing first.

Neal proved as expert at oral and fingering techniques as his pal. Didn't they say they'd gone to school together? Well, they must have excelled in this lesson—top of the class.

Speaking of outstanding, while Neal made me come several times with his mouth and fingers turning me into a gibbering pile of mush, Charlie kissed me. I stroked his outstanding, upstanding dick; my fingers only just wrapped around it, as it was girthy as well as long.

It was never my intention to make him come too soon—I wanted to suck him and feel it fuck me—but when I drew my palm along it for the umpteenth time, he shuddered and jerked. The wet evidence of his orgasm caught me by surprise as it splattered against me.

Perhaps it wouldn't take him long to recover?

Charlie used his discarded T-shirt to mop up the mess, and I looked at Neal, who had sat up, eyes wide, and his lips looked full and red.

"Do you guys have condoms?" I asked. "Because I have some in my bag." I hadn't expected anything to happen when I left the hotel for a drink, but it was always best to be prepared.

For a moment, I thought I saw a panicked expression flash across Neal's face, but I must have imagined it. It wasn't as if he could be a virgin or gay. "Do you like sucking cock?" He sounded almost timid as he asked in a small voice.

"Are you kidding?" I wouldn't say no to anything after what he'd done for me. He didn't need to ask twice. I got up on my knees before him. My mouth was ready for both of them, and I wondered if double-entry oral was a thing.

CHAPTER THREE

A Norse warrior captured me at Dalston
Malka Selby

MUCH LATER, IN THE late afternoon, I left my hotel room. It was so much later than I intended for my trip to Stoke Newington, but I didn't want to put it off for another day.

The distance from King's Cross was only about three miles, as the crow flies, but there was some awful rush hour traffic, which meant I could have walked there in less time than traveling by London Transport.

It was dark by the time I got off the bus at Dalston and I'd still only covered half the distance. I had to walk a couple of hundred yards to the next bus stop. I considered completing my journey by foot from this point, and I was undecided. The fresh air and exercise would be welcome and, therefore, tempting. It would give me more time to mentally prepare, as well as enjoy all the Halloween decorations in the windows on the route.

Who was I kidding?

I had no idea how to prepare myself.

I hadn't been back to the house since my mother was arrested. At school holiday times, I'd been one of the few kids who stayed at school, along with the children from overseas, or I had been shipped off to a residential summer camp, or I'd stayed with friends, AKA Betty and Louise.

I didn't even know why I was going to my former home. Uncle Byrne lived there now, but it wasn't as if he was expecting me. He'd shown no interest in me all the years I'd been away. He'd never visited me at school nor invited me to stay with him. He was just my legal guardian: my reluctant, uninterested, distant guardian, that was all.

I stood to gain my independence and access to a hefty trust fund on my twenty-first birthday, in just a few days' time, so pitching up unannounced just before then seemed like the right thing to do. I had no idea what I was going to say or what his reaction would be.

Technically, I didn't need to see him at all. Technically, the lawyer told me that I owned the house and could evict my uncle if I wanted to. I didn't. I had no reason to have anything to do with the damned house. I wouldn't need the money, and I intended to place my roots somewhere else.

I had only gone a few hundred yards along Kingsland High Street when my feet left the floor and I flew backward. I traveled a mere few inches before a plate-glass window halted my momentum.

My brain hardly registered the angry shouting only a few feet away as I slammed against the nearest vertical surface and was held helplessly pinned against the glass by a muscular mountain of maleness.

It was a wonder I hadn't noticed him on the street minutes before he grabbed me. With his wild Viking looks, long golden locks, and great height, he would have stood out from the crowd on the busy London shopping street.

His solid, broad body pressed against me. His crazy-green eyes, flecked with yellow and gold, gazed into mine. I didn't see him before, but now this man had my full attention.

Making a mental note of his striking features in case I should need to give a description or pick him out of a police lineup, I concluded my attacker reminded me of a long-haired and youthful Norse God Thor, particularly a version played by actor Chris Hemsworth. Although this stranger's hair was longer and more golden, strawberry-blond AKA ginger. So the whole Chris Hemsworth connection was more wishful thinking.

If any man had to grab me in the street and press himself against me, I just wanted it to be Chris Hemsworth. Or one of his brothers. That's all I'm saying.

For the briefest fraction of a second, a fantasy about the sexual chemistry between myself and a Thor-look-alike flitted about my brain. It was shooed away by the fact that this man had just assaulted me, and it wasn't over. My feet weren't on the floor. He held me aloft and invaded my personal space.

Obviously, he hadn't read the memo about keeping away from me, the daughter of The Black Widow. A warning that I might be as dangerous as my mother. My mother's nickname didn't come from the Marvel comics but came from the spider connection; she gained it after killing a bunch of men. It was a brutal knife crime.

It occurred to me that I might want to take full advantage of my anonymity and sleep with all the gorgeous men who looked like Viking warriors while I could before they found out about my crazy mother. A story guaranteed to put any man off me.

Thinking about sleeping with a stranger who'd just accosted me wasn't my first inappropriate thought of the day. There had been so many; it was just how my brain worked. It must have been the aftereffect of the threesome that started the night before and had continued into that morning.

Waking up between two guys on a hotel floor after a night devoted to orgasms and oral sex multiple ways certainly inspired sexy mental meanderings.

"Shush," he whispered in a low voice.

What? Dazed and breathless, no matter how lewd my thoughts, I certainly hadn't voiced them aloud.

Gorgeous looks and Scandinavian background notwithstanding, there was no excuse for manhandling me and then shushing me without introductions first.

Winded, gasping for breath, I didn't call out for help, which would have been the obvious thing to do. Too shocked to fight back, I didn't knee him in the groin. It wasn't an option anyway, because my trapped legs were squashed between a solid man and shatterproof glass.

Biting his ear seemed to be the only avenue of attack open to me.

I added earrings to the mental description of my assailant. Several earrings. All different. All silver. A hoop, a little stud with a red jewel, and one of silver threads fashioned into a geometric shape. I blinked and looked away, unwilling to be reminded of the torture of mathematics lessons, which taught me the now-forgotten names of those damned shapes.

Even though I was held against my will in a vise-like grip, at that point I wasn't overly worried about my predicament. I felt inexplicably safe. A man couldn't just accost a woman in a crowded public place like Dalston and expect to get away with it.

It was late afternoon or early evening, take your pick, depending on the time of day you get up. I'd not been awake long, so I'd opt for late afternoon. The autumn sun had set a while ago, but the streetlights, the traffic, and the shopfronts ensured Dalston was bright and well-lit, busy and bustling. People surrounded us.

The ginger stranger had a sincere face. He didn't look like a pervert, and if only you could tell by looking, there wasn't any inappropriate hard-on pressed against me. And believe me, we were close enough that if he had any erection of note, I'd have known about it.

I seemed to dangle there for a long while before I processed what was happening to me, but it probably took two or three seconds.

"Shield," he whispered.

What?

Only because Thor held me aloft could I look him in the face and even consider his ear within biting reach. More importantly, I caught a glimpse over his shoulder.

Behind him, a group of men passed by. They appeared agitated. The reason for that may have been to do with the man at the center of the group who wore a loud 1970s retro shirt. It wasn't the dazzling shirt that made me believe he was at the heart of the commotion. It was the huge fucking machete that he waved above his head as if it were a harmless flag or banner on a protest march.

The men shouted at each other, arguing in a language that I didn't understand, Turkish, I'd guess, given we were in Dalston and its local population. I couldn't understand a word of it except for the one word, the frequently used expletive.

On my travels, I'd discovered *fuck* and *taxi* are two words that are the same in any language and used all the world over. These men weren't hailing taxis.

Thor and I weren't the only people squashed against the storefront.

A silent huddle of men, women, and children held their breaths as they stood petrified in a compact huddle. Using their bodies to hide and protect their loved ones, adults held on to youngsters, burying their innocent faces in clothing so they wouldn't see.

Turned to the buildings, people stayed still and quiet, trying to make themselves small and invisible. I knew what they were all thinking, because I had the same idea. They hoped they wouldn't attract the attention of Retro Shirt. Collectively, we tested the magic we'd all learned as kids when hiding from a monster under the bed covers: if we didn't see him, he wouldn't see us. By the same token, if we didn't look at the sharp blade, it wouldn't find us.

I realized the immense wall of man-muscle might have just saved my skin. His broad back, more or less, hid my body. He continued to offer protection while, like the other people, he didn't look back.

Shield? Is that what he'd meant?

I looked beyond my human shield.

Some people called out. "He said he's going to cut his head off," one voice shouted. Others said things about bloody bloodsuckers and washing the streets with blood. It was all far more bloody graphic than I wanted to hear.

Thanks for the translation, but TMI.

Although even I knew the translations weren't verbatim, because I heard frequent fucks in every sentence.

No one needs the F word translated. But if they didn't translate his sentence accurately, how much could I trust in the translation at all? There was a big difference between *going to cut their heads off* or *cutting all your heads off*, minus the fucks. Only slight changes in the words, but resulting in vastly different meanings. If he was just going after one specific person, then I needn't worry. Obviously, I wouldn't condone his intentions, but at least I didn't face imminent danger.

As things stood, I didn't know if we stood in the path of danger or who was the intended target. But whatever, Thor stood between me and everyone else.

In English, in an incongruous cockney accent, Retro Shirt shouted in my direction, "I'm going to fucking cut his fucking head from his fucking shoulders."

Plenty of fucks there made him sound proper cockney.

Finally, fear took hold. My mouth went dry, and my stomach felt like that sharp blade had sliced through it.

The ground trembled, as it often did in London. That always seemed magical. I accepted the rumbling under my feet was only ever caused by a passing truck or an underground train. We didn't have earthquakes or volcanoes in England.

I shut my eyes, hoping that Retro Shirt didn't focus on me. And if I couldn't see him, he wouldn't see me. *Wouldn't it be great if there was such a thing as invisibility magic and it worked that way?*

I'd only been back in the country of my birth for twenty-four hours, and it had been nonstop eventful. Wild dogs on leads, my first threesome, machete man. Whatever next?

When the sound of the shouting moved away and I sensed the people around me beginning to breathe again, I opened my eyes.

People scuttled away, whispering and holding on to their family members.

Thor stepped back and lowered me to the ground.

Not usually stuck for words, I was at a loss after sharing such a scary and intimate moment. I should say something like thank you for protecting me, and I liked your enormous body squashing all my soft bits.

Thor didn't look at me; however, instead, he looked all about, up and down the street and across it, everywhere but at me. He didn't allow me to say anything. "You're safe for now," he said in a low whisper. Then he walked away without looking back.

Stunned and confused, I stood still and watched him pace off toward Stoke Newington, the same direction as I should've been going, except I just stood still in a daze. The real-life human Hagrid who'd always tower above most people wouldn't disappear into the crowd soon. I'd bet he got fed up with being asked if he played basketball and if he'd reach up with those long arms to rescue kittens out of trees.

A sudden gust of wind blew my hair across my face, and a gentle hand landed upon my left bicep, distracting my attention.

"Are you all right?" Clad from head to toe in black leather biker gear, the young woman who spoke looked vaguely familiar, but I wasn't sure where from. Not here, that was for sure. I hadn't been down this road for almost fifteen years.

She had black hair and tanned skin. She might have been Turkish, but I shouldn't assume everyone around Dalston was from that country.

"Yes, I'm fine." I wasn't. I was in shock. I needed to work on a better response to such questions if things like this were going to keep happening. "You should check on the kids, not me."

Of all people, I knew from first-hand experience that children shouldn't be confronted with the reality of knife crime. They shouldn't be aware of people being hacked to death, even less see such a monster as that man making terrifying threats.

Realistically, I was the last person who could offer support at a time like this. The event stirred up my childhood memories in a way that I didn't want to deal with right then.

Though I didn't see the murders with my own eyes, I'd grown up haunted by stories of people stabbed and decapitated in frenzied knife attacks. It was all too close to home.

Ignoring the woman and everyone else, I glanced back in the direction Thor had taken. He'd disappeared from view. That was what I needed to do too. Get the day back on track. It had already begun late enough after last night's impromptu party.

Incredibly, my threesome buddies hadn't snoozed after they come for the first time; they'd insisted on staying up throughout the night. We'd chatted, and drank, and kissed, and more. When I thought I couldn't stay awake any longer, one of them would go down on me, an action guaranteed to wake me up. All in all, it passed as a very pleasant night of sleep-deprived erotic torture. It had been well into the day by the time I left the guys and went back to my room to catch up on much-needed sleep.

The consequence of my late night meant I had a late check out from the hotel. I then deposited all my worldly goods in a couple of bags in a left luggage place next to King's Cross station. I wasn't sure whether I'd stay in Stoke Newington with my uncle, check into another hotel in London, or take off on more travels again.

It all resulted in my trip to Hackney taking place in the evening instead of the daytime as I'd intended. If I'd have been earlier, I would have missed that bit of excitement.

Keeping the children close, many of the adults were scuttling away. Other people around me talked on their mobile phones, and I overheard enough to discover at least one person called the police.

There wasn't any practical way I'd be helpful by sticking around. The police wouldn't need my account of what happened or a description when many other people around me seemed to know the knife man's identity. I heard them muttering names in their conversations. My staying there was pointless. And on top of everything that had happened over recent days, it drained me.

"Good."

I looked back. The woman who had spoken to me raised a crash helmet and pulled it over her head. She looked cool in her leather outfit with her gleaming motorbike beside her and her unfazed attitude.

Her motorbike rested right by where she stood, which was along the path that machete man had walked, so she couldn't have been parked there through the traumatic event. She wasn't there when it all happened, yet she'd stopped and spoken only to me. I didn't know where she'd come from or when she'd arrived, but apparently she was leaving.

Strange.

I needed to calm down and take five minutes out.

I couldn't go from this incident directly to face my past head-on. I shuddered. I didn't like to think about how I was raised in my early years sharing my former home with the woman who was to become a notorious brutal mass murderer: no matter how many years had passed, and no matter that she was my mother.

By luck, I found myself standing outside the perfect place to regroup before making my way back to the house that held so many memories. And in need of a drink, I headed into the nearest juice bar.

CHAPTER FOUR

The Red Berry Delight of the Kingsland High Road

Varu Vasile

MY TEETH ACHED. IT was early evening, and I hadn't had a bite to eat.

Tantalizingly, she walked right up beside me and pulled out the next stool at the counter as if she didn't know what I was. Didn't know or didn't care.

Interesting.

She was no more human than I was.

Well, perhaps a little more human than I.

She had a pulse, for a start. And strangely enough that pulse was racing as she entered but even as she approached is slowed down.

"What are the chances?" The rest of the thought stayed inside my head: *Of a woman like that entering my space.* What were the chances of a witch like that approaching me without trying to kill me as if I posed no danger to her?

Yet, here she was, alone and pretty much harmless and defenseless, from what I could tell.

"Pardon?" Sitting down on the barstool, she turned to look at me. "Did you say something?"

"I wondered why of all the juice bars in all of the towns in all of London town you had to walk into mine?"

Her eyebrows raised in disbelief. "Yours? This is your juice bar?"

"Why shouldn't it be?" The question was a test. Did she know who I was? What I was? Would she tell me that vampires don't do cafés, restaurants, and bars?

"You're about my age." She shook her head. "I suppose you don't have to be old to run a juice bar."

I smiled. So we were going to play that game. Pretend we were both mundane. Pretend we were of a similar age.

"I'd guess you're twenty, coming up to twenty-one. And I'm just a tad older." *Tad older by hundreds of years, poppet. And the youth of today don't say tad, do they?* I kicked myself for the error. And they didn't call each other poppet. Keeping up with modern languages was such a bore. "And if the Dalston Smoothie Shack wasn't mine, why else do you think they'd let me sit in the prime seat at bar, here, without a drink?" I waved my hand across the clear countertop in front of me.

The cafe wasn't mine, of course. I threw out the challenge to test her reaction.

Out of sunlight, I could sit anywhere I damn well pleased. As an aged elder vampire, I possessed powers that witches could only dream of. Powers that should have meant she stayed well away from me, if she knew what I was and what was best for her longevity.

I am a little arrogant, I will admit. And I have earned the entitlement to be arrogant.

"What can I get you?" Chris, the bartender, interrupted our conversation.

"Um, I haven't decided." She stared up at the chalkboard behind him.

Chris reached out to pick up a laminated menu, but before he handed it to her, I tendered my suggestion.

"May I recommend the Red Berry Delight?" There were few things lovelier than watching the rich, red liquid wash around lips and the residue settle around smiling white teeth. Of course, I wanted to watch her consume a drink the color of fresh blood rather than something like mown grass or, even worse, warm sunlight.

My purpose for visiting the Smoothie Shack was one big ulterior motive. This was the best place to pick up an early evening snack, even for a blood-sucking vampire, because healthy-juice drinkers had the sweetest vital fluid flowing through their arteries.

I hadn't expected the scintillating scent of the blood of a powerful young witch to come so close to me, the provocation almost more temptation than my hungry teeth could take. How delicious would she be? I imagined taking her right there and then, before she could find some way to disable me.

Merely the way this witch's bouquet teased my olfactory cells was almost as pleasurable as draining the blood of a virgin.

You didn't find many adult virgins in East London these days, at least not one without a chaperone.

The last time I stumbled across such a delicious smelling stranger, he was a young virgin and a witch. And that bloomed into a wonderful ongoing relationship. I doubted if I'd be so lucky to begin a similar relationship with another witch within a decade of meeting Beck Colborn. A meeting which, by coincidence, also happened right here in Dalston.

Typically I'd come to expect a century to pass before I'd meet a new treasured friend like Beck, although there was one other in recent times. That relationship came to a tragic end a mere couple of decades earlier.

A virgin's blood is hard to resist, and the temptation is nigh on impossible to resist when it is the blood of a virgin elemental witch.

Beck tasted every bit as good as he smelt, and there weren't many vampires who'd ever been fortunate enough to sample such a rare treat.

"It's her first time in this place, Chris—make it a Red Berry Delight on the house." I worded my request to suggest I was in charge of the place.

And in a way I was; it was the natural way of things. Powerful vampires are in charge when we want to be. It didn't matter that I didn't own the Smoothie Shack. I compelled Chris to carry out my bidding whenever it suited me. It was one of my useful skills.

"My treat. Now, while Chris whizzes up the fruit-filled delight, tell me why you're here?"

"For a smoothie?" Her eyes examined me intently. "I mean, a drink. Obviously, what other kind of smoothie could I mean?" Her cheeks colored a little, and the subtle change in her scent also gave her away. She was flirting with me, but she stayed calm and at ease. In fact, her heartbeat stabilized at a steady rhythm indicating she was perfectly relaxed.

Curious.

Few witches in her seat would remain so relaxed sitting next to me. It was as if she didn't know I was a vampire.

The usurpers, humans and witches together, persecuted my kind because they feared our power. If she were any other witch, she would have recognized me, turned around as soon as she'd entered, and put as much distance between us as possible, hoping I wouldn't track her and kill her. Or she'd have pulled out a weapon and threatened me.

Many a vampire hunter had fancied their chances and tried it, and yet, my undead form still graced the night.

There were two feasible explanations for her composure. First, given her young age, she might not yet know about me, or second, she didn't fear me because of who *she* was.

Possibly, of the two of us, I should be more concerned.

She radiated great energy such that I'd rarely sensed before. Before she'd entered the Smoothie Shack, I'd sensed her massive aura moving closer. I'd been aware of her since she'd entered East London. I hadn't felt a presence like her since... well, I'm not sure I've ever known a presence like hers.

One day, if she lived long enough, she'd be a powerful woman. A witch of the highest order, I reckoned. But she hadn't tapped into her potential yet.

"I mean, tell me why you're here in East London? Do you live around here, or are you visiting someone?" I asked.

"I've been traveling abroad, and I've just arrived back in the UK, and I'm on my way to visit my uncle." She smiled innocently. "What about you? You have an accent, and I'm wondering if it's from a place I visited. Where are you from?"

I had a story I'd pull out for such chit chat. "I'm from Romania." We were doing this. Pretending we were ordinary, mundane mortals having a casual conversation and knowing nothing about each other. "My family came here when I was just a child, but I held on to an accent. My name is Varu, by the way, Varu Vasile. And welcome to The Smoothie Shack."

At that moment, Chris placed the creamy red drink before her. "Enjoy. It's complimentary," he said and ignored me as if I wasn't there.

It was difficult to tell if a mundane like Chris had any awareness of the powerful, wild, aura surrounding the witch. Humans sometimes seemed to sense things, but most of the time, they were such simple creatures. The way they called themselves rational always made me laugh. And I realized I was showing a smile to my new companion. Teeth retracted.

"I'm Malka." She lifted her smoothie to her lips.

Malka: I knew it.

This was not the time to say *I knew your parents*. After a few moments in her company, I recognized this young witch. Now probably wasn't the time to tell her she smelt like Serina Selby and had something of the look of her father about her.

I remember when you were a babe in her arms. And now you've marched right up to me the same way humans do as if there is no danger at all in approaching an ancient, hungry elder vampire.

She smiled with a trace of red berry juice beautifully coloring her lips, and she reminded me of her handsome father. “Varu? Is that a Romanian name?”

“Yes, short for Varujan.”

It wouldn’t do to have the heiress to the House of Selby mistake me for one of the Turkish mob. I wanted to make it quite clear who I was, and who I wasn’t.

If Malka lived long enough, one day she’d be far more powerful than her mother, and Serina was a fifth-order air witch so not to be trifled with. Although I didn’t rate Malka’s chances of survival all that highly. Not if she continued traveling around London after dark with her aura on display, letting every vampire and demon for miles know what she was. It was like a teenager advertising a free-for-all party on social media. Her aura acted as a calling card to her adversaries.

And then there was the way she sauntered up to this particular apex predator as if she had a death wish. If I were any other vampire, she’d be facing her final minutes right sitting beside the beast who would kill her.

It was a wonder the Turkish vampires hadn’t drained her powerful blood as soon as she stepped foot on Hackney’s streets without letting her get this far. I could only guess that the kerfuffle following the death of a subjugate had distracted them for a while.

The humans were on the rampage, led by a grieving father who wanted answers and revenge. Not that people in modern times had any grip on the ancient skills and knowledge needed to depose vampires.

And it was only just after twilight.

If vampires weren’t the masters of concealed movement, I’d probably detect them gathering in the nearby streets, ready to avoid the mob and grab the elemental witch.

It wasn’t just the vampires everywhere who were a threat to her, either. As we spoke, witches were most likely plotting the downfall of this young upstart.

I wouldn't let that happen. The Selbys would never forgive me, and they were my powerful allies.

I gazed at Malka in wonder.

If not for her dear mother, then I'd do all I could to protect her out of respect for her father.

If sweet little Malka pulled her tribe back together and took control of her seventh-fucking-order potential, the witches of Summer House Road might become the most powerful coven in all England. Imagine that. Frankly, I didn't get my hopes up. I'd been walking the earth for long enough to know there was no certainty in anything.

"I will escort you to Stoke Newington if you like. Make sure you get there safely."

And I caught the little flutter of her heartbeat: a sudden change as her pulse raced. Sweat broke the surface of her skin, and I smelt her fear.

All perfectly normal reactions when mortals recognize me for what I am. I was used to it, and still enjoyed it. You see, fear has a more complex bouquet than mere indifference.

A seventh-order witch of the House of Selby had entered a room that I occupied, she'd approached me and sat next to me, as calm as you like, with no sign of stress. But when I suggested walking her home, she had a meltdown as if she'd be safer on her own. Dear Dracula, she did not understand the order of things in East London, or who her friends were, that was for sure.

"I never said I was on my way to Stoke Newington." She raised the glass to her lips and sipped.

Didn't she? Didn't she tell me that was where her so-called uncle lived? Of course, I'd suspected her humble childhood home was her destination. She hadn't told me.

Awkward.

But she wouldn't be here on Kingsland High Road if she were going to any other Selby property.

"No, you didn't." By the luck of the devil, I had a workaround for this corner I'd gotten myself into. "I'm the one going to Stoke Newington. I live that way. If you're going in that direction, I can escort you, is all I meant. Of course, if you're off to Hackney Marshes, then we'll say our goodbyes here."

Her heartbeat immediately slowed as she relaxed. "Do you know, oh, hold on, let me check the address again." She pulled a scrap of paper from her pocket. If I were alive, I'd bet my life she already had that address memorized and she merely carried the slip of paper like a comfort blanket. "Summer House Road in Stoke Newington?"

Of course, I knew it. But I feigned astonishment anyway. "No way. It can't be. I reside on that street too. What are the chances of that?"

Her heartbeat raced again. I'd overdone the theatricals and said the wrong thing. Damn it. She thought I'd made it up. I should have told her my address first. From her point of view, it seemed suspicious that I declared I was going to exactly the same place as her after she mentioned it first.

There was no digging myself out of this. I wasn't certain about the so-called uncle. My guess was it was an easy way to refer to her legal guardian. That would be Fire. He was the obvious choice for her mother to appoint as guardian, and he resided in her home, but he was no more a blood relative than I was.

If I said a mass murderer had lived near me fifteen years ago, Malka would know I referred to Serina Selby. But it was hardly the way to reassure her that I was someone safe to walk home with.

"Sorry. Phone vibrated," I explained. Pulling out a mobile phone, I went with Plan B. "You know how they interrupt all the best plans." Referring to my phone as 'they,' I tapped on the screen, careful to angle it away from her.

"Not really. I don't have one."

I jerked my head up. *Even I live in the twenty-first century these days.* "How do you survive?" I asked in amazement.

"I get by. I'm just unlucky and always manage to break them, pretty much as soon as they come out the box. I'm hopeless with technology. But I've found plenty of other things my fingers are good for." Her eyebrows raised a little and her head angled to the side, ever so slightly.

Oh, my. If the young lady's innuendo was an attempt at flirting, it widely missed its mark. I was too old and too dead to be turned on by thoughts of anything she might do with her fingers. Her blood, on the other hand, that would get me stiff and aroused.

The phone thing was news to me; I didn't hang out with witches enough to keep up with how their magic meshed with modern technology. Unless it wasn't a witch affliction, just her own unique problem. Perhaps Malka regularly had awful luck.

I looked at my phone and focused on my own plan. "Something has come up, and I am, in fact, destined in another direction." I stood, making obvious my intention to leave. "I hope I'll catch you another time when you're in Hackney."

"You're not going straight home?" The relief in her voice was severely misplaced. If only she knew how much danger she was in and how my companionship would bring her safety.

"I will be home before the morning, but right now, I must depart in a different direction." Nevertheless, I would not let her travel through London alone and unguarded.

"So, to answer your precise question, no, I'm not going straight home." *I will shadow you all the way until you are safely on your land.* "But it is a straightforward walk from here. You can't get lost. Straight up that way." I pointed north. "Turn left at Church Street, and then your road will be on the right. I live at the very far end by the cemetery. Feel free to call by any time."

And with your own best interests and life prospects at heart, you should be begging me to stick close by.

CHAPTER FIVE

W*ho was she calling a virgin?*
Malka Selby

FOR SOME REASON, WHEN he stood up to leave, my eyes worked all the way down his body, and I hummed my approval—audibly hummed.

"Hmm." *Yummy.* "This smoothie tastes good, by the way. Excellent choice. Thanks." I said, trying to cover up the fact that I'd been purring. I didn't understand what had come over me. I wouldn't mind him coming over me, truth be told. That happened once, with those guys the night before, and suddenly I could barely think about anything else.

"My pleasure, Malka. I hope to see more of you again soon."

I'd like that too. To see a lot more of you, of course.

I tried to drag my thoughts back from my mental art gallery of scantily clad men.

It wasn't as if he could detect that my panties were much damper now than when I entered the bar.

He couldn't possibly read my mind. And yet, I couldn't help imagining he'd given me a knowing wink.

The temptation to turn and watch him leave proved irresistible. I might have glanced over my shoulder, no more than three times, to check him out.

Nice arse.

There goes a man who should have a bright neon warning sign over his head saying *cute guy alert*. He had everything: the charm, the looks, and even his own business. He was just about my age, easy on the eye, and easy to talk to.

However, he had a strange turn of phrase. He spoke like a crumbly, old grandparent, not a guy of my age. Perhaps that reflected our different backgrounds. I was English, and he originated from Romania. It made little sense, though; I was the one who'd been brought up among wealthy girls in a stuffy, old-fashioned boarding school, and him? I assume he'd grown up around here, on the ethnically diverse streets of twenty-first-century East London.

Living on the same street as my house, no less.

Go figure. As he would say, *what are the chances*?

If he lived at the end of the road, where he said, I'd run into him again, even if I had to arrange for it to happen—accidentally on purpose. And if he didn't live there? If he was lying, it was just as well I didn't go off into the night with him.

The sort of strangers who talk to you in juice bars will surely be all right. I imagined bad boys hung out where there were drugs and alcohol, not wheat-grass and coconut milk. There was nothing about Varu that seemed dangerous, apart from his all too good looks, his perfect complexion, and spiky black hair adding to his charming confidence.

I could do with a friend or two like him.

Some hot, charming, young guys to show me the night-life and a good time. After all, we wouldn't live forever, and there were so many men and so little time.

At twenty-one, almost, I ought to get out more. Why not pick up a guy who hangs out at a place serving smoothies? At least he should have a healthy attitude toward life and women.

Much as Mr. Tall-Dark-And-Handsome was a very pleasant and much-needed distraction to the issue of knife-wielding maniacs on the streets, death by stab wounds, and worse, I didn't have the time to dwell on him or any of the earlier disconcerting incidents of the day. I had a house to visit and my inheritance to check upon.

The berry juice proved the perfect pick-me-up energy boost and just what I needed before making my way to the house of my childhood.

I remembered it though I hadn't been back since the night they arrested my mother. I was curious to see how much had changed. I'd lived there until the age of seven, when I had a brief spell in foster care before being sent to boarding school paid for by my family's wealth. Even though I didn't know my father—he died before I was born—and my mother was in prison, my family estate could still afford a privileged education.

"Cheers," I mumbled and raised my glass in a silent toast to absent friends.

My future hung in the balance.

Going back to the house was the first step in figuring things out.

A blood-red fruit drink and flirting with a handsome guy was what I needed to put myself in a positive frame of mind to face my old home. He might not have noticed my attempt at flirting, because I hadn't much practice in the art of seduction.

When your mother was a crazy mass-murderer who butchered an entire crowd of men, and you spend your formative teenage years tagged as the daughter of London's Black Widow, it doesn't do wonders for your dating profile.

As soon as I reached eighteen, I left school, glad to leave behind everyone who knew about my history. I'd been wary of getting involved with anyone while traveling and working abroad, where English wasn't the first language. I'd had fun and experiences, and I'd seen some of the world, but I'd been guarded too.

Refreshed and ready to face whatever I would find at my old home, I drained the glass, left the cafe, and headed north.

The walk to Stoke Newington may have been a mile or more from Dalston Junction. I could have caught the bus, but I covered the ground on foot, and barely noticed the journey as I was lost in my thoughts. Although it was early evening and dark, the streets at night were as busy as in the day; London is a twenty-four-hour city.

It was reassuring to see so many enormous men in black uniforms as I walked past the police station on my left, especially after the earlier incident.

When I neared my destination, I became more aware of people milling about. They seem to back away, clearing the path before me as I approached. I worried that this was some figment of my delusional mind, and I was going as crazy as my mother. Why would people notice me or move for me any more than they would pay attention to anyone else? It made no sense.

When I reached the junction with Stoke Newington Church Street—where I was supposed to turn left—and I was within a few hundred yards of my old home, a gigantic figure emerged. I wanted to go west onto Stoke Newington Church Street, but he blocked my way so I couldn't change direction without crashing into him.

"Keep going," he murmured in a hushed whisper. He turned to walk beside me, keeping me heading north. "There's a riot about to break out back there. It's too dangerous to go that way. Follow me for the safe route."

There was a sincere urgency in his tone, and I didn't doubt him. Why would I? This was the same man who'd previously held me against a shop front and saved me from a possible beheading. I had no reason to fear him and some small reason to trust him.

I sensed that I wouldn't be able to walk fast enough to move around him or get away, but if I slowed down, he would too.

We walked together quickly.

A sense of urgency rolled off him, so much so it tempted me to run.

We hastened our pace. After we'd covered only a couple of hundred feet, he clasped my arm. "We can cut through Abney Park."

Having not lived in this area since the age of seven, I didn't know where he was talking about. I'd looked at a map earlier but had no alternative routes committed to memory.

Just after we passed a parade of shops, he steered me toward a park that was set back on our left. Impressive stone pillars supported tall black railings, and the central gates stood wide open.

"This way." He beckoned me to accompany him into the park.

Only a short stretch of grass was visible beyond the railings, and after that, just a few trees stood out from the dense darkness. I hesitated. It wasn't the sort of place to enter at night with a stranger. "I'm not sure this is a good idea."

"Don't be afraid of what's ahead," a familiar voice with a slight European accent whispered in my right ear. "It's what's coming up behind that you need to fear."

Apart from the giant on my left, I hadn't realized anyone was so close to me. I certainly hadn't heard Varu approaching. I heard Thor's heavy footfalls to one side, but Varu must have worn some of the latest silent-technology sneakers. I had to wonder if I was going deaf in one ear. I still heard traffic, cars, and buses moving along the road, and the wind rustling through the trees.

"You?" I said.

"No. Not me. What's behind me is what you need to get away from." He grinned as if he'd said something funny and not at all menacing. "We need to move, Malka."

Varu sped up as we entered the gate, he walked ahead of Thor and me.

A glance over my shoulder confirmed, sure enough, many people were following us. I almost stopped still in surprise, not expecting to see a bunch of emos getting closer. They wore big boots with sharp, shiny buckles, studded belts, and shiny chains. Their clothing should have jingled and their footsteps stomped as they moved, yet I hadn't heard them at all. I had no idea how they'd gotten so close without making a great noise.

Suddenly, a bright light shone ahead. When I glanced to my side, Varu was holding his phone in front of him, illuminating the path through the trees ahead.

Thor had saved me earlier, and I had no reason to distrust Varu. Decisively, I chose to trust these two men and go along with their plan, although approaching dark woods accompanied by male strangers seemed reckless and crazy.

We entered through the open gates and hurried toward the woods. I practically ran to keep up with the two tall men moving toward the dark forest ahead. "What exactly are we running from?"

"Trouble," Thor replied.

We didn't reach the trees before trouble caught up and surrounded us.

We turned, and I gasped. The sudden appearance of the menacing goths seriously freaked me. I had no idea how these people had gotten all around us without me seeing or hearing them approach. I was so freaked that I felt comforted by the fact that Varu and the Viking-like stranger were on either side of me, even though that was a weird coincidence.

A woman moved close to Thor. "Fire, I've no quarrel with you, but you can't keep her."

Her gaze wandered over him like he was a delicious meal on her plate, and she couldn't decide which part to bite first. Was she a jilted or jealous girlfriend? I didn't know the guy, but I felt a pang of jealousy.

Get off my hunky Viking and find your own long-haired love.

Another woman stepped forward. She dramatically sniffed the air. "Don't give her up peacefully. I don't mind drinking virgin blood." The goths shared a sinister joke based on humor I didn't understand.

Virgin!

Who was she calling a virgin?

I might look young for almost twenty-one, but I'd lost the V-card a few years earlier. Now I'd even done a threesome. Okay, so strictly speaking, there was no penetration when I had that threesome, but the guys were all into oral and lots of it. That must count.

I had no idea what woman the goth girls were talking about. However, if they referred to me, then they misread the relationship between the red-headed giant and me.

Ginger Thor took the tiniest step toward goth-girl number one. "You know I can't let that happen. You must come and present your requests in the proper fashion." That was a fucking weird thing to say; sounded a bit like this couple was into BDSM role play.

The other girl sneered; I didn't blame her.

She was a lanky emo with long, greasy hair and a squashed face. "A race who'd stab us in the back while we sleep will never get that respect. You don't deserve it. Here's our offer to you—give her up, and we'll let you live."

Let him live!

It was laughable.

He was twice the size of those nutty women, but they had a backup army of ghostly faced goths behind them. They had the numbers, but honestly, most of them didn't look like they'd be able to punch their way out of a paper bag, and certainly not take on the god of thunder.

"You wanna taste me?" Thor stepped toward them. "I'd never give up one of ours."

What the fuck does that mean?

I wasn't on top of London street talk.

Varu stepped closer to me so that his arm rubbed against mine. "Look, I know you're not acting for yourself. You will put decades of peace in jeopardy, and for what?" I noticed the almost-permanent smile had disappeared from his face, making him seem much older and serious, for once.

"This isn't about us, Varujan." Both women stepped closer.

Silver glinted in a flash of movement so swift that I only attributed it to Thor after the fact.

Both women crumpled to the ground before I saw the blade—two blades. Beside me, Thor transformed into a terrifying rage. His arms swung around. It dawned on me he was the person with the knives and had slashed these women down.

I would have screamed, but even my scream was so terrified that it had fled the area ahead of me. I simply stood petrified with my mouth open. I couldn't bring myself to look at the bodies on the ground.

There were more goths, emos, punks, or whatever they were, standing behind the two who'd taken the first hit from the madman's anger, and I didn't want to see the next target for Thor's rage. I thought he'd moved toward them.

At the same time, Varu grabbed my arm and urged me to turn and run.

He didn't need to tell me twice, but I didn't move instantly; terror paralyzed me. Varu had to pull me to get me started.

"Run, Malka, to the left." Varu dragged me away, and, at last, my legs responded. We made toward the dark trees. We ran together. He stayed by my side. I didn't question it.

I didn't want to consider what would happen if angry-Thor chased and caught us after we'd seen what he'd done. I didn't want to be the witness he took down.

It was only my second day back in London, and twice I'd seen up close its reputation for knife crime.

Running forward, I charged ahead of Varu. I heard no noise behind me; it was as if I was running on my own. I didn't want to look back—it would slow me down—but I was aware Varu was on my heels because of the light he held, presumably from his phone. He shone it on the ground ahead of us so we could see where we were going. The path split in many directions, and without hesitation, I ran to the left as earlier instructed. "Run left," Varu had said.

From further back, I heard more footsteps, so I just kept going as fast as possible.

Varu must have been super fit as he wasn't even panting. There was no thud on the ground as his feet hit the trail, but the light stayed steady as if he was out for an evening stroll.

"You can stop now," he said after a short distance. He didn't even sound out of breath.

I didn't want to stop, but I couldn't keep sprinting like that. Cramps and burning leg muscles left me with no choice. I'd be dead if this were the zombie apocalypse. I'd seen *The Walking Dead*, and I knew the monsters kept going.

Worryingly, I heard footsteps getting louder and with no hint of slowing, and I had to know. Glancing behind, I made out a large figure at a distance but gaining on us. He might have brought danger. After witnessing the big guy who saved me from a knife attack earlier slicing into two women, I didn't know what to expect next or who to trust.

Hiding seemed an excellent plan. I made the snap decision to veer off the path and take cover behind a tombstone. If Varu didn't shine his light on me, hopefully whatever trouble followed us would go right past. If I were lucky, Varu, who wasn't out of breath, would keep running and lead the big trouble away from me.

In the shifting shadows, I weaved between the toppled tombstones, stumbling over soft, uneven ground littered with tree roots and pieces of broken gravestones. Of the memorials still standing, they were tightly packed side by side and back to back.

Foolish Varu kept his light on me and followed me. "I'm trying to hide," I growled.

"Stop. You can stop now. You're safe," he said, and I sensed him stopping as the light ceased bobbing about, and he didn't follow me.

All before my feet was blackness; I took the final step. I stubbed my toe against something hard and fell on my hands and knees into the black ground. That's right. Into the ground, not on to it. It was like landing on a sponge cake that was cooling, fresh from the oven. Around the exposed skin on my hands, the earth felt warm and dough-like. The force of my landing pushed a hole straight through the firm crust.

My hands and knees were both enveloped in the mulch mix of the earth. Naturally, I tried to push myself up, but there was nothing to push against. I hadn't reached right through the cake mix to the bottom of the tin. Instead, my arms and legs slowly sank deeper into the moist, soft ground.

It turned out Varu wasn't the gentlemen I'd thought, and instead of coming forward to help me out of the mushy earth, he just watched me sink into it before turning to the big man who approached him. As I sank faster, it occurred to me that perhaps Varu didn't see that I'd fallen. He'd turned the shining light away from my direction. He probably thought I was hiding. Whereas, in fact, I was falling.

The true extent of my predicament didn't become clear to me until I was more than half-buried in the soil and decaying vegetation. I could have called out; I should have called out, but my brain froze in fear and confusion.

Within seconds I'd slipped so deep that only my head rose above the surface. I saw the red-headed murderer talking to Varu.

I kept falling.

Both of them were oblivious to me becoming buried a short distance from them.

My mouth filled with dirt when I finally opened it, too late to scream.

CHAPTER SIX

Twas just another night in the cemetery for a humble and evil vampire
Varu Vasile

LEAVING THE PATH, FIRE crashed his way between the gravestones, making enough noise to disturb the dead.

With nothing other than moonlight and the ever-present glow of London night-life reflecting back from the clouds, I directed the beam of light from my phone toward his feet. "I don't know why humans have the expression' *blind as a bat'* when bats can make their way perfectly well at night. Whereas you're likely to fall and break something if it wasn't for a friendly vampire nearby holding a light for you."

Fire grunted. "Where is she?" Bewildered, he looked all around at the darkness surrounding him.

By the time he drew up beside me, the young witch had disappeared from view, leaving a collection of accessories behind as evidence she'd once been there. I could see them, but Fire could not, of course.

"Well. Well. What are the chances?" Chuckling, I couldn't hold back the broad smile from my face.

"What did you do with her?" He pulled out one of his knives. If he'd meant business, he'd have drawn two. He was no match for me, at least, not whilst it was nighttime. Nevertheless, I took a few steps to the side. Unlike the young Turkish vampires he'd attacked, I was prepared for Fire and his lethal silver weapons.

I had the advantage over him of speed and centuries of experience. And I could see in the dark, but I wasn't about to underestimate him.

"Don't threaten me, Fire, if you don't want me to kill you. I looked after your young witch and got her to safety, even though she's perfectly capable of looking after herself. Meanwhile, you've attacked my kind on our doorstep, which creates another mess I'll have to sort out, so you can put your shiny silver toys down."

"You move too fast anyway," the fire witch mumbled as he sheathed the knives yet again. That was a good sign. He wasn't set on making any attempt on me.

"You only managed to strike those vampires at the entrance to the park because they didn't expect it. They were foolish to underestimate you, Fire. They don't know you as I do." I thought it an opportune moment to stroke his ego a little.

When they had gotten close enough, the young vampires' senses merely told them that Fire was a witch, and when they moved close still they realized he was a virgin and possibly an elemental; all factors which meant his blood was prized.

They wouldn't discover the extent of his power until they were within inches of him, because he'd mastered hiding his aura so well. It was easy for them to underestimate him. And they wouldn't have know about his training and very particular skill set.

I had gotten close enough and known Fire long enough to know much about the power and abilities of this witch.

Those foolish, young vampires didn't have experience of fighting witches or vampire hunters. The thousand-year witch wars should have taught us all how brutal and ruthless witches could be. They exploit methods of trickery, deceit, and would stab us in the back whilst we sleep.

Daylight is always another enemy.

The war was ongoing, but the local truce had been in place for more than a century and made many young vampires complacent. They didn't expect to meet a witch armed with silver blades, willing to attack and finish them off. They weren't familiar with the Summer House Road coven.

If they'd have known Fire as I did, then they'd realize he despised vampires and needed little provocation to strike first. He was more powerful and better trained than most modern witches because of how he was raised. And this girl was more precious to him than anything else in the world. He'd die for her.

Her safety was important to me too, and that was one of the few things that united myself with this miserable witch.

"If you've hurt the witch, Varujan, you won't live long to regret it."

We're doing first names now.

"I wouldn't hurt the Selby daughter, Haydn. My intention was also to protect her, didn't you notice? She's important to you and your coven."

"You knew who she was?" He tilted his head. His heartbeat had slowed down to a normal pace. As everything about him seemed to be calming, the likelihood of him rashly attacking me subsided.

Of course, I knew her. I didn't respond aloud to his ridiculous question.

"If she's safe, then where is she?" he asked.

For his benefit, I shone the light of my phone on the spot where she'd vanished. I'd seen her go. "You have a powerful earth elemental for your coven." Satisfied that we'd looked at the scene of her disappearance for long enough, I walked forward and bent over to gather up all of her belongings. "What are the chances?"

"Chances of what?" he grunted. But his body tensed, giving away his surprise at my declaration of her element.

"The chance of many things, dear Fire witch. Of the Selby daughter being so blessed with such a rare gift. Of her already using her significant power to pass through the ground. That magic isn't for beginners, you know. And hasn't she heard of natural fabrics?" I held up one of her lacy undergarments.

Green eyes fixed on the cream-colored brassier for a moment. "She's not even twenty-one. She can't have powerful magic yet."

I shrugged. "I'm just a vampire. What comprehension do I have of your magic?"

"Don't give me that, vampire. You just said she used her great power as an earth elemental, which is impossible. She's had no training, and she's too young to have mastered it alone. Or did I misunderstand you?"

Perhaps it wasn't wise for me to share all my knowledge. I decided he didn't need to know just how powerful she might become in the future. "She was here. She's passed through the earth of her own volition and is now in an underground chamber. Make of it what you will. No vampire took her below ground, the little witch did it herself." I wrapped the largest garment around the smaller and tiny items as I gathered up all of her belongings. Fire watched me work, which was fair enough given he couldn't see in the dark whereas I could. "She still has much to learn. When I travel through the earth, I take the clothing too."

Even as I nonchalantly gathered the lady's clothes, I kept Fire under surveillance. His temperament was as fiery and unpredictable as his element, and he was a skillful master of those silver weapons. "As for her potential, I've already seen her aura. She will be powerful if she learns how to use magic. But then I might be wrong. What do I know about witches? Whatever you choose to believe, it makes no difference to me. I'm just a vampire telling you what I've seen."

Fire knew I wouldn't be making shit up, but he'd just had a run-in with vampires that probably shook him.

"How are we going to get her back?"

"I don't need her back." My eyes met his glare. "Are you asking for my help again?" I was evil. Why deny it? I enjoyed the push-pull relationship I'd had with Fire over the years since he'd come to live within my territory. He'd never liked me, for some reason, which I found impossible to fathom.

By any measure, I am incredibly likable.

"You made a promise to her mother." He scowled.

In other words, no, *he* wasn't asking for my help; it was our absent mutual friend, the girl's mother who asked for my help.

"And for that reason, I'll now take you to the young witch below ground."

He crossed his arms over his chest. "How?"

Much as he tried to appear calm in a controlled macho way, I perceived his nervousness. My acute senses detected all his little tells, the change in his odor and his heartbeat. His apprehension amused me.

Did I mention I am an evil vampire?

"The most direct route will be the fastest. I'll take you through the earth, the same way she went. I can take you, and you can keep your clothes on. And I'll take her clothes too." I held them aloft.

"If she used her magic to pass through the earth, why did she leave her clothes behind?"

"You're always telling me you witches are naturists. Perhaps that's why she's now completely naked underground."

Fire huffed, as I knew he would. I found it easy and fun to provoke him every time we met. Too easy.

"Having an interest in nature isn't quite the same thing as nudism, vampire. We work with nature and maintain harmony. The natural order of things isn't something an undead monster would understand."

"No need to get personal, hot head. You may well be glad to call upon someone with superior predator senses like me from time to time." I snapped off the light and plunged him into darkness. "Don't forget, I've only been holding this light for your sake. I can see perfectly well without it."

I laughed. To anyone who overheard, it might have sounded like a row between enemies, but for us, we usually spoke to each other this way. Like football supporters or construction workers, this was our own mode of robust but friendly banter. We would be far more polite and circumspect with our real enemies.

Damned if I was going to share all my knowledge with him or any witch. I knew why only her body had passed through the soil. She was a novice magician and hadn't mastered the advanced magic required to carry other items with her through the earth. It was a miracle that such a young inexperienced witch passed through at all. But that must have been down to her seventh-order potential.

"You should know not to underestimate me."

A patrolling fox snapped a twig nearby; the fire witch jolted and looked over his shoulder with some alarm.

"Don't worry. No vampires have followed us." *At least, not yet.* "To take you below ground, I must wrap my arms around you. I will do that now, so make sure you keep your silver away from me." I'd already kept a watchful eye on those weapons and was certain they were tucked well away so that I wouldn't come into contact with them. Just touching their surface would be enough to sting like a bastard.

"Okay," he grumbled. The dark still blinded him, but he was never helpless.

"Don't worry, even though we'll be close, I won't bite." I couldn't resist adding, "Not unless you ask me to." Oh, yes, that might be one of the reasons he didn't like me. I smiled to myself, thinking about the many meanings of my words.

"I'll never ask you to bite me, vampire. Never." He spat the words out as if there could be nothing worse than my bite and nothing more insulting than the word vampire.

"Such a shame. You'll only ever wonder what you are missing." And a shame for me too; I wouldn't mind tasting Fire.

What he thought he knew about vampire bites might not be entirely accurate. He'd learned from myths that a vampire bite was always seductive or fatal, or both.

He'd been taught to despise vampires as wicked monsters.

But his opinion of me, in particular, may have been tinted by the fact that we shared a love for the same one man. And I drank from Fire's lover from time to time. He wouldn't admit it, but I suspected Fire harbored some misplaced green-eyed jealousy. It really was needless; I would not steal any of his beloved witches away from him.

Fire and Water both claimed their relationship was nothing more than a friendship with benefits. If they believed that, they were delusional. It did have benefits, but it was clearly much more. I didn't need my acute vampire vision to see the two men cared greatly for each other and appeared to be in love.

If I had a heart, watching those two men in denial about their true feelings for each other would break it. It was all because Fire had been saving himself for the future High Priestess of the Summer House Coven. I was sure the former High Priestess never intended such devotion to an absent leader and the denial of romantic happiness for Haydn when she secured his commitment to her daughter.

The lives of mortals are short. Witches are mortal. I believe they shouldn't forgo happiness but seize every opportunity to bask in it. They don't generally consult me for advice on how to live their lives.

My face squashed against his cheek, close to the rich food fountain running through his veins. I didn't dare think about testing his fiery virgin elemental blood whilst wrapping my body around his and about to take him through the earth.

When my nose filled with the scent of elemental blood, my fangs descended in anticipation.

"You might want to shut your eyes and your mouth for this," I warned him.

CHAPTER SEVEN

Officially dead and right pissed off about it
Malka Selby

THE MORE I THOUGHT about it while sitting in the dark on the gritty floor, the more pissed off I became.

What a fuckin' load of shit day this is turning out to be.

One moment I was walking through the streets of London, and still on a bit of a high from the multiple orgasms of the night before and those that followed in the morning. The next moment I was chased through something allegedly called a park, but what turned out to be an overgrown forest with toppled gravestones stacked higgledy-piggledy between the trecs. It wasn't so much an inner-city wildwood as an inner-city graveyard with trees and ivy. Correction, it was straight out of a horror film. The sort of place I never thought existed in real life.

Whether I tripped over a gravestone or a protruding tree root, I wasn't sure, but the result was the same. I'd fallen and didn't stop when I hit the ground. At first, I thought it might be boggy marshland, but it wasn't wet at all; the earth was a powdery dry mulch.

It was the weirdest sensation. I kept sinking deeper and deeper into it. It terrified me. I thought I would drown or be buried alive. When it reached my nose, I shut my eyes. The soil entered my ears and my nostrils. It seeped under my clothes and closed in around my body, damp and dirty against my skin. Moving through this gritty material was every bit as disgusting and suffocating as one might imagine.

I must have left my actual body lying in the dirt above ground, and it must have been my soul or spirit or whatever that fell through the ground into hell.

Of all the weird things that happened today, dying had to be the worst.

I was officially dead.

And a bit pissed off about the whole dying thing.

The ground swallowed me up, and when I landed in hell it hurt, which didn't seem fair either. I'd imagined that once someone died, they'd stop feeling physical pain.

The injustice of finding myself going down below didn't sit well with me. Admittedly, I could've prayed more in life, but I didn't think I'd been all that bad.

Then there was the big question. Why did I have to die? Varu and I outran the crazy, big, ginger guy with the knives. He was the one who started cutting people up in a London park.

Presumably, if I'd been a better person when I was alive, I'd have flown upward. I'd have liked to try flying. That was just another thing to piss me off; landing in hell meant missing out on the flying up to heaven experience.

Instead, naked, I fell through into a vacuous space and sat where I landed with dirty stones digging into my bare arse. Clothes didn't accompany one to the afterlife, apparently.

My sense of touch still worked; I still had the same body, just without clothes.

Either I'd lost my sight in death because I couldn't see my hand in front of my face, or not a single photon of light existed in this black hole. I'd expected hell to be warmer and bathed in the pleasant glow of firelight.

The pitch-black darkness disorientated me; I couldn't work out which way was up and which way was down. I concluded my arse sat on top of something.

Tentatively, I overcame my dread, stretched my arms out to either side and slowly waved them all around. There was nothing to touch within arm's length. Not even a goddamn creepy spider's web. I didn't dare stand up or move in any direction in case I fell into goodness knows what next.

Even without a welcoming party, this had to be the afterlife. I'd just been buried alive. If I was alive, in a dark cavern, underground, and no one knew I was here, my prospects were grim, and I was as good as dead.

I didn't feel calm at all. I felt very, unbelievably, overwhelmingly, fucking stressed.

"Hello. Is there anyone there?" I heard the telltale hint of panic in my voice.

Surely I'd never been so terrible as to deserve an eternal sentence of existing alone in a vacant dark pit.

I'd been in this pitiful predicament only a few minutes, and I was well on my way to having a full-blown freak-out. Would my panic attack last forever? A noise interrupted the silent crisis—a dull thud.

Something had dropped to the floor right beside me.

I reached out.

I found thick, soft fabric covering a leg, a calf protected by denim.

"What's that?" The male voice sounded a little freaked, but he didn't move.

"Me." A mere feeble, scared, squeak substituted for my normal voice.

I moved as close to him as possible, so my face rubbed over the denim. The scent of smoldering charcoal surprised me; he smelled like he dropped in from cooking food over an open fire. Never had a familiar scent and denim clothing been so reassuring.

Desperate not to let him go, I feared that if I stopped touching him, he'd vanish, and I'd be left alone again for the rest of my death.

My hands went upward, ironing over the denim jeans.

When I reached bony knees, it became apparent that I'd stroked my hands over a thick muscular calf.

I continued my way up his strong and unmoving legs. I needed help to keep my balance and stand up in the disorientating darkness, and I aimed to use this surface to guide me up from where I sat on the floor.

My hand grasped thick and solid thighs like tree trunks.

Just when I'd reached somewhere that I wouldn't have touched if I were still alive and could see what I was doing, his hands wrapped around my arms and pulled me up into a standing position. It was dark, and I was dead, and I had nothing to lose, so I felt anyway. I find out he was well proportioned—all over.

Standing and unable to see anything, I buried my head against his chest and, robbed of sight, I drank in his masculine wood-smoke scent. Evidently, he stood much taller than me. His arms wrapped around me, and that would have been his first clue that I was at least topless.

It may not have been the time or the place, but cuddling up to this man in the dark, I was aware of my pussy becoming a bit wetter.

"Malka, is that you?" he asked as I pushed my body closer to him.

"Who else would it be?" a familiar male voice with a European accent answered. I didn't realize anyone else was in this dismal place with us.

Without seeing him, I sensed Varu smiling.

I released my grip on the big guy as I recognized the scent from the last time he held me. "Thor?"

"What?" he said.

Of course, he didn't know his nickname.

"Yes, it's her." Varu chuckled. "Reunited at last, and a touching scene. Oh, but you two can't see it. Here."

"Oh!" For a few seconds, I looked away from the direction of his voice when a bright light dazzled. I guess we all did the same.

When my eyes became accustomed to the light, I focused on Varu. "How come you two are wearing clothes?" I demanded.

He looked me up and down with no sense of propriety, but Thor only glanced in my direction and turned away once he saw my lack of clothing.

"It's customary across Europe." He smirked and held out a bundle that I recognized. "Here are yours; you left them behind."

"It wasn't intentional. I've got no idea what just happened."

"When we'd stopped running because we'd reached our destination, you didn't stop but carried on going straight down. I waited behind to bring this lump through, as most witches don't have that kind of magic."

I pulled myself away from the Viking and held out one hand for my clothes.

Varu handed the pile to me.

I grasped them and held them in front of my stomach, wishing they'd instantaneously get right back on my body where they belonged, seeing as they'd come off so easily.

There was no point in trying to cover anything; it was too late for that, they'd seen everything, and trying to hide would only make me seem more vulnerable than I already was in this confusing place. I wasn't about to step any further away from these men and the light than I had to. To be honest, naked or not, I'd have liked to cuddle up in between the two of them for safety.

What happened to my clothes? How come you are both still wearing yours?

The injustice of it. I wouldn't have objected for one minute if death had treated us equally and presented these two naked before me. Especially after what I'd just handled while it was cloaked in denim.

Thor coughed and glanced at me. "How did you do that, Malka?"

I was still naked, and he looked away.

"Do what? I did nothing, but tell me, how do you know my name? And, in fact, who are you and what the bloody hell is happening here? And why are you always around when awful things happen? Which isn't true because lots of awful things happened when you aren't around, but why do terrible things happen when you are around? And why did you kill those people? It's all because of you I'm dead."

The men looked at each other, and there may have been eye-rolling or just confusion on their faces.

"Do you want to get dressed so that Haydn will be able to look at you whilst he gives you answers, and so that we can get out of here?" Varu continued to stare at me, as if he didn't want to miss a reverse striptease. "And then we can all go and eat."

At the word eat, Thor, apparently named Haydn, grimaced in Varu's direction, crossed his arms, and looked agitated, but he said nothing, and he still didn't look at me.

"Is watching me get dressed your idea of a good night's entertainment?" I asked Varu.

"No. Not at all. I'm looking forward to what comes next. I want to watch Haydn explain to you who he is and how you came to be here."

"I don't have all the answers, Varu. I don't understand why she's holding her clothes instead of wearing them."

"Because she hasn't put them on yet," Varu snapped at Haydn.

Without caring that Varu watched my every move, I dropped the bundle on the dirty floor and picked my way through it. I pulled on my panties and then my leggings. At least with my bottom half covered, I felt more like my old self.

While I dressed, I wondered what Viking-Haydn could have to tell me that interested Varu. Varu obviously knew more than he had ever let on.

I was dead and way past caring what another dead person did. Or thought. Or looked at. Or how they looked at me. Although a part of me found it a little thrilling to be naked in the company of two hunks. And the way Varu watched me, well, it was sort of arousing. Who knew women still got wet down there after death? Not that I'd admit it. Varu didn't need to know, and so long as he didn't put his fingers to my girly parts, he wouldn't find out how wet I was, right?

It wasn't so easy to conceal arousal if you were a guy. I didn't know why I hadn't thought to look sooner, but after looking down to sort out my footwear, I looked up straight at Varu's crotch. There was no evidence of excess blood flowing there, so perhaps he wasn't watching me for pervy kicks after all. I was a little disappointed.

Once I'd pulled on my shoes, I felt ready to kick ass. And even more prepared when I'd gotten my top on, too.

"Haydn, huh? So that's your name. Again, why was I naked, and you two weren't?"

Varu chuckled. "I've been able to pass through the earth for centuries. I can bring things through with me. It's not something witches can do, usually, and not something you've mastered yet. Still, with training and practice, you should be able to do it too."

"Oh, for fuck's sake," I rarely swore, but this day had tested me to the absolute limit. I'd bet everyone swore when they woke up dead. "You two are a right comedy double act." Dressed and decent, I stood up and put my hands on my hips. "So, answers. Tell me what you know."

Haydn looked at me at last. His eyes ran up and down my dressed body briefly before he said, "Let's get out of here and home first."

"Right you are, then; this way." Varu turned and led us along a corridor. Who elected him the leader of our dead exploration party? But the man held a flashlight, and he gave me clothes, so I was prepared to cut him some slack. I wasn't going anywhere without him.

"Are you always smiling?" I asked him.

"I haven't had this much entertainment since you were a little girl."

Death had clearly sent him mad, and it was my turn to roll my eyes.

"I can't help enjoying the irony," he continued. "Here I am, long since dead, and I'm the one with the perfect eyesight. You two would like to think you're superior with your regular heartbeats, your bad breath, and your meals consisting of salted solid food. Yet, you can't be trusted to operate a light on a smartphone. Oh, yes, it all amuses me."

"Fucking smart arse," Thor-Haydn murmured. He and I were on the same wavelength, all right.

"You're welcome to hold the phone if you want to, Fire. I don't need it," Varu held out his hand, offering it first to Thor, who shook his head, and then to me. "Only, earlier this evening, Malka told me she doesn't have a phone because they always break. Correct me if I'm wrong, but I believe you suffer the same problem. Fire, do you want to explain why the two of you can't use phones without breaking them?"

He shook his head. "Later. I want to get above ground and somewhere safe first."

I sighed. I hadn't a clue what the men were talking about but feared death had messed with their minds even more than mine. As my mother was criminally insane, I'd spent my entire life watching out for signs of madness in myself and the people around me.

I would not get any sensible answers in this dark cave, and I wasn't sure the earth above us wasn't about to collapse, bringing down the remnants of the corpses buried in the graveyard upon our heads.

Varu led the way.

Although the light from his phone was bright, he kept it shining on the floor, so I didn't get to see the walls and ceiling. At least my feet found a safe and solid place to step.

Thor-Haydn and I followed. I had the impression Haydn didn't know where we were.

I should get used to calling him Haydn if we were about to spend the rest of damnation together. Though I didn't understand why I should be sentenced to my eternal death in hell with a murderer.

And I still didn't understand why the men kept their clothes whereas I lost mine. More to the point, why they'd seen me naked but hadn't returned the favor. Maybe that would come later, and I wouldn't object. They had promised us a lot of debauchery in hell.

If there was any justice in the world, I'd been good enough in my life to deserve at least two naked men in my afterlife, surely. Still, as dead companions go, these two didn't look too bad in their clothes, either.

We wandered through a labyrinth of underground tunnels, but I focused on my feet landing on solid ground, step by step in front of me. Eventually, that ground changed from dirt to terracotta floor tiles.

"We're in my house," Varu announced. "And if you don't want to go up the same way you came down, then you must climb. Now, shield your eyes."

I did.

And just in time, because he must have flicked a light switch.

"Wow. A ballroom," I gasped.

The bright light from a chandelier illuminated a magnificent, opulent space like something from a Cinderella story with a central staircase leading up to balconies on either side.

Haydn looked equally impressed as he gazed about the room.

"This would be the place for one hell of a party." I laughed at my joke, but the men both looked at me as if I spoke a foreign language. "A party in hell, below ground? Get it?"

Blank. No sense of humor.

"After the old summer house was demolished, this was built on the site," Varu said, proving that I wasn't the only one who can make statements that seem to come from nowhere.

"The summer house? Are we underneath Summer House Road?" It occurred to me.

"Yes. I had this built underground before they constructed the modern street."

"Those old houses have stood for two hundred years; I wouldn't call them modern," I protested.

"Malka, please don't get him started on what is modern. Trust me on this. You will regret it."

“Anything post-industrialization and urbanization is modern,” Varu stated with all the confidence of an expert in the history of architecture. He pointed to the far end of the room. “The stairs. These are for making a grand entrance, of course, but beyond the door at the top of them, there are about three hundred and eighty-seven steps to take us up to the basement level.”

“About? Three hundred and eighty-seven steps sounds a very precise number.”

Varu winked. “Let’s go.”

CHAPTER EIGHT

I *might be dead, but the men around here are dead fucking crazy*
Malka Selby

THE ASCENT FROM HELL was via a steep, narrow, winding staircase.

The men insisted I led the way, which I suspect had something to do with whoever followed would be at eye level with, and inches from, my backside. The guys jostled for that position.

The endless staircase went on and on. If I'd counted the steps, I'm sure they far exceeded the few hundred which Varu had mentioned. I couldn't believe we'd fallen so deep into the ground. We had to be making our way up to heaven via the inside of a skyscraper.

Gasping for breath like an asthmatic, I paused to rest on a half-landing where the staircase wrapped around on itself, and there was a door to god knows what.

"Do you think this is the stairway to heaven? And if so, are we nearly there yet? Because if we have to go much further, I'll need hooking up to pure oxygen," I said with gasps for breath as punctuation.

Haydn also breathed heavily. "It's taking us up to Varu's house. No, I wouldn't call that heaven."

Varu wasn't breathless at all. The man must've been super fit. "Come now, Fire, you've heard stories. Some visitors have found a little bit of heaven in my home, and that's why they continue to return time and time again." He winked suggestively.

Haydn huffed, crossed his arms over his broad chest, and glared hard at Varu. "Heaven, huh? That's not what I'd call it." Momentarily I envisioned Varu going up in flames, as if Haydn's anger alone could do that.

"I can see you guys have some bad history. But it doesn't matter. All history's in the past. We're in this boat together, and we've got to get along with each other."

"I've done all I can for that vampire," Haydn grumbled.

I raised my hand. "Don't call each other names. I'm not listening to another critical word against Varu, who has done nothing wrong. It wasn't him who just killed a couple of women in the park." Before either of them said another word, I turned away and started the ascent again. I noticed Varu snickered as they followed.

It only took a few more bends in the stairwell, and we ran out of stairs.

Unfortunately, four blank walls and no door surrounded the top landing. I silently wept inside at the possibility we'd climbed all those stairs for nothing. We'd passed many doors on our way up, so it wasn't as if we'd have to go all the way back down again.

Varu came and stood alongside me. He pushed on the flat white wall. It moved, gliding away from him as if it were on wheels.

"Nice concealed door," I commented in surprise.

"Thank you. Glad you like it." Varu led the way through, and we found ourselves standing in the very ordinary hallway of a house. The front door was just a few feet away, and a blurred street light and the inky night sky were visible through a frosted-glass panel. For the first time in hours, things appeared normal.

"Welcome to my twenty-first-century home. I wasn't expecting company, but you're welcome to stay."

"We'll not stay. I can take it from here, vampire." Haydn went for the door. Poor guy didn't seem to realize we were dead. It wasn't my place to tell him. I had enough trouble coming to terms with my untimely and tragic demise. "Thank you for bringing us back to civilization, Varu. I want to take Malka home."

Clearly expecting me to follow Haydn, Varu stood aside to let me pass.

I placed my fisted hands on my hips, feet fixed squarely in place. "If you think I'm going to follow you blindly into the street, think again. Why should I go anywhere with either of you? I don't know where the fuck I am, but of the two of you, I'd rather stay with him." I indicated Varu with my thumb. "At least, so far as I know, he hasn't killed anyone."

Haydn's face was a picture; it looked as if I had slapped him with a wet herring.

Varu's eyes widened, and he swallowed hard. His shoulders jerked up and down, and his hand went to his lips as if trying to stifle a laugh.

"All I know about you is that you look like a red-headed Viking, you bring trouble with you, and despite it being illegal, you walk around London carrying knives. I'm staying with Varu."

Orange flecks appeared in Haydn's storm-cloud eyes, and more than ever, he looked like Thor, the god of thunder. "Malka, I'm Haydn Bryne. Does that name mean anything to you?"

It did.

"The Haydn *Byrne?*"

It hadn't occurred to me that this stranger was Haydn *Byrne.*

I'd imagined the person who bore that name to be much older, grayer, and altogether less fit than the Haydn standing before me.

"Haydn *Byrne*. My uncle?" I hadn't seen him since I was a child.

"I'm not exactly your uncle. I'm your legal guardian, or I was when you were younger. You were on your way to see me when we took that diversion, weren't you?"

As far as I was concerned, this unexpected piece of information fitted the pattern of the unexpected events that happened that day. It had all been fucking crazy. "Diversion? You just killed two women out there, and now we're dead. You call that a diversion?"

Haydn's brow furrowed, and he looked at Varu, who shrugged his shoulders and smiled back at him.

"We're not dead, Malka," he said after a minute of silence. "I live in your house, which is across the street from here. Your mom made me the trustee of your estate before she went on her mission. Come home with me now, and I'll explain."

"Wait one minute. Mission? Do you mean that killing spree? My mom called it a mission? And you knew about it?" Dread, fear, or anger seeped through my veins—I wasn't sure which, but a lump formed at the back of my throat to go with the rock sitting in my stomach.

"When you were seven, and I was eighteen, we put all the paperwork in place so that I'd look after the estate."

Varu soon watching, looking mildly amused and as if none of this sounded like alarming news to him. These two men were both crazy. Dead crazy. It was the only explanation. The worst thing was that they both stood between me and the front door, and I didn't want to run back down those stairs.

I weighed up my position. Haydn appeared the more menacing of the two men, and he stood poised to leave. He was in denial about the death thing. I understood that. But he was unhinged and unpredictable, with a fiery temperament. It seemed lucky I found out his true colors sooner rather than later and hadn't turned up at the house alone when I was still alive.

"Guardian, uncle or not... I see what's happened since I met the two of you, and I'm staying here for now, with Varu."

"With a vampire!" Holding his hands out to the sides, Haydn looked aghast. He hadn't expected rejection. With his handsome features, I doubted he experienced it often.

"Stop calling him names."

The two men exchanged knowing looks, as if they had an unspoken conversation.

Varu shrugged. "You're welcome to stay too. Talk here."

Haydn took one more look at my face before addressing Varu. "Take care of her until the morning." He opened the door. "I'm trusting you, Varujan. Bite her, and our truce is off. You know I'll kill you."

Varu laughed. "You can try, but it's too late for that."

At least he acknowledged our death. Haydn seemed to believe life would continue as normal.

Haydn's comment only confirmed the wisdom of my decision to stay put. He was one crazy fucked-up piece of work. And a murderer. Perhaps he was cut from the same cloth as my murderous mother. Together they conspired to give him control of my well-being just before she was locked away for being mad, bad, and dangerous to know.

"I don't understand how you've lived this long," Varu said to me once the door had closed behind Haydn.

"What you mean? You know we're all dead, right?" I must have banged my head, but I had no idea what killed these guys. They followed me so quickly. It could have been those punks, the friends of the girls Haydn killed.

"Whilst I certainly am and have been for hundreds of years, the two of you are very much alive."

CHAPTER NINE

Sometimes one has to rethink everything
Varu Vasile

ONLY AN APPALLING JUDGE of character would have thought they were safer with me than with the fiery witch. Even I'd admit that, and I'm no fan of Haydn Byrne.

Much as I reveled in the knowledge that I excelled at entrapment, giving off the wrong signals and luring women into a false sense of security, I had genuine concerns about the safety of this young witch. She wasn't my prey. Her lack of instinct for self-preservation was a problem for all of us in Summer House Road, myself included. Of course, she was oblivious to the risks.

Lingering by the door, Fire deliberated on his next course of action. I almost saw his brain whirring. I'd seen many people with that same expression of confusion, but usually, that was after they'd forgotten that I'd just drank their blood. He was unsure whether to leave her with me.

Like a true pal, I helped him decide what to do next. I invited him to stay, so he decided to leave. I knew he would. We'd never warmed to each other, which was ironic seeing as he was Fire, Mr. Heat, a fire witch, and I was stone cold dead. Deep inside, he would have known she was safe with me.

He left, and I closed the door and bolted it because you can't be too careful.

"Which do you want first, the bathroom and the guest room or food and drink?"

"Neither. What I want are answers. How do you two know each other? Do you know those women he knifed? Did he kill them? And why did he do that?"

"Come and sit with me, Malka. I'll show you your house." I led her through the first door to the front room.

"Start with what's wrong with that guy. He's so delusional." She chattered away as she followed me, oblivious to all the implications of our movements. I'd rarely turn my back on a witch, and it was unusual for a witch to be in a vampire's house after dark voluntarily. Of the witches, only my closest trusted friends would ever drop in on me.

We passed by the small dining table used by the mortal family that lived in this part of the house. I sat in one of the two chairs by the window and invited her to sit in the other. It was a place I rarely sat. Why gaze through a pane of glass instead of being out there interacting with the world? Unless it was daylight, in which case it would be far too bright for me. In the daytime, I stayed beneath the house.

"You need to rethink everything you thought you knew."

"You're damn right there. I never thought the afterlife would be like this, for a start."

After hundreds of years on the planet, I finally had the chance to tell someone they weren't dead but alive, and the job turned out to be more difficult than I'd have guessed. "This isn't the afterlife, not for you."

"So, what is it then?"

"For some reason, your mother wanted you to have a normal upbringing; she wanted you to live as a mundane child."

"My childhood wasn't all that ordinary. I spent it at expensive boarding schools and dreaded anyone asking about my parents. I suffered a fair amount of teasing for being the daughter of a nutter. I've often wondered if she'd have sent me to boarding school even if she hadn't gone to prison." Malka appeared wistful.

"You're not descended from the Nutters. To my knowledge, that family has a separate northern-based lineage that has never mixed with yours."

She looked confused as she focused on me. "What would you know? You can't know my mother. Did your parents tell you this? Are they home?" Malka turned toward the still-open doorway.

"There's so much to tell you. Let's just suppose I did know your mother. I've known your grandmother, and many members of the Selby family and their friends. I've met people who knew Alice Nutter, but I never had the pleasure of meeting her myself. I remember these houses being built and the house that stood here before. I've been alive for hundreds of years."

I saw her laughing at me.

"It may seem hard to believe, but why not? You had it in your head that we three were all dead when we were underground. Why should that be any easier to believe than what I'm telling you?"

"I passed through the earth and into an underground cave. Death is an excellent explanation. Well, not good; in fact, it's terrible. But it does the job of explaining things."

"And what if magic is a more accurate explanation? Your magic took you through the ground. You're a witch. Haydn Byrne called me a vampire because I am a vampire. He always means it as an insult, but I can't be offended by a statement of fact. He's a witch, and you're a witch. You both have the potential for powerful magic."

It would alarm most people to discover they were sitting chatting with a vampire, but Malka took it in her stride. She tutted and huffed out a big breath, not taking me seriously. "I can't do magic."

"You can do great magic; you just aren't cognizant of it yet. Few witches can travel through the soil. You're an earth witch, which is pretty rare. And Haydn couldn't follow you. He doesn't have that ability."

She twirled a piece of hair around her fingers. “You both came through the earth. How did that happen?”

“I brought him. It’s something vampires can do. We have an affinity with the earth, but I’ve known very few witches that can do what you did today. You haven’t been raised with your kind, but my experience tells me you have the potential for substantial power.”

“Okay, so you’re crazy as well. I guess death does that to you.”

“I can’t argue with that. I’m a vampire. I’m dead, and I’ve been dead for centuries. You may assume we’re about the same age, but you’d be off by several hundred years.”

She shook her head, and I heard a low murmur, “Horse shit.”

“That’s your house.” I pointed through the window to the house opposite and then moved my hand horizontally in a straight line. “And the one next to it is also part of your estate, and the one next to that, and the one next to that. And so on.”

Her eyes widened in surprise. “I didn’t realize my family owned so much property. The lawyer never told me that.”

“You have a lot to learn about your family, and Fire—I mean Haydn, of course. He is well placed to tell you. But as you’ve sent him away, there are a few things you should know. Indeed, you need to understand as a matter of some urgency if you’re to live to see another day. Firstly, and this is most important, I pose no threat to you, I assure you, but other vampires do.”

She sat looking as cool as refrigerated fruit, but I sensed her tensing. Every change in mood accompanied a change in scent detectable to creatures like myself. So far, she wasn’t out and out frightened, but apprehensive. It was a shame. I preferred some of the other more enticing erotic aromas she’d expelled earlier.

“Prove it. Prove any part of what you’re saying is true.”

“It doesn’t matter to me if you believe it. I have no vested interest in your life except that your family has been good to me over the years. We’ve watched out for each other. I would hate to disappoint your mother and ancestors if I allowed something bad to happen to you." *And I would do anything for your late father*. "And right now, negative forces are amassing close to here. You may well fall in the crossfire of whatever trouble is brewing."

I pointed to her house across the street. "Those boys over there, on the other hand, they are very interested in your well-being. They do care about you. I'm not the best person to explain witchcraft to you, but Fire will be willing. He's been eagerly waiting for your return."

"Boys? Are there more like him?"

"There's no one quite like Fire, but there are more witches in this street who will take care of you. And you do need to learn to look after yourself because the war between witches and vampires continues. We have a local truce here. But it is on the brink of collapse, and the way things are turning, we'll both be at risk from vampires and witches."

There was so much I couldn't tell her. So much I hoped she wouldn't ask. So much she needed to learn if she were to survive.

"It's a fine story, but I want proof. If you're a vampire, show me sharp teeth. Or the coffin where you sleep."

"You've seen enough proof already. We've all passed through the earth. You've seen what's below this building. I sleep behind one of the many doors we passed."

She pursed her lips. "But shouldn't you live somewhere more fancy than here if you're an old vampire? Shouldn't you be loaded and living in a castle or country mansion or Kensington?"

"I did. I have long resided hereabouts on the Abney Estate. This was a well-to-do area way back when the Abney and Fleetwood estates were sold to create the non-denominational cemetery, I acquired a share of the land with your ancestors. I remember it well; it was just around Christmas time almost two hundred years ago."

"Two hundred years ago. Is that when you came to England?"

"No, the old estates were sold in 1838. I'd already lived in this area for a long time by then, including in Abney House itself for a while. Since that time, vampires have come from all over the world to be entertained in my underground ballroom, which you've seen. Everything I need is here, including security and ample supplies of food."

"Is it true that vampires need to sleep in a coffin filled with earth from their native lands? Or is that just in Dracula films?" She asked some good questions.

"My old friend Dracula. He is, of course, completely fictitious. I have a great fondness for the many Dracula films, and for Bram's books. I spent many an hour right here in Stoke Newington talking about Romanian myths and vampires with Bram. He was fascinated. I had no idea, at the time, that he was pumping me for information for a novel, but I was delighted with what he produced. Have you read it?"

She shook her head.

"The way he blended fact and myth within his imagination was marvelous. You know he was Irish, don't you? He'd never set foot in Romania, but he captured the atmosphere well in his Gothic horror story. The result was rather good, though; I've also never been to Transylvania."

"And sleeping?" Her question halted my rambling chain of thought.

"Do I ask you about your sleeping arrangements? No. I'm not interested whether you sleep with one witch or many, or if it's someone different every night. But as you ask, vampires don't have to sleep in coffins and don't have to sleep in the earth of their native country, but they may choose to do so. I'm rather partial to Romanian soil myself."

"You think you can tell the difference between British and Romanian soil?"

"Now, that is an interesting question with an interesting answer. Yes, of course. The soil is flavored with the blood of whoever died or was buried there. You can eat what they ate and experience their death when you immerse yourself in soil. I can feel the fear, anger, and sadness that seeped into the soil in the final moments of a person's life."

She leaned forward, fascinated.

"I see the war that killed them, or sometimes I'm disappointed to find the ground is comprised of the bodies of people who slipped away peacefully in their sleep. The local soil around here tastes of dissenters, non-conformists, and revolutionaries. It's rich in the blood of Quakers and witches who were buried side by side in the cemetery." I pointed to the wall—beyond it lay the place where we'd passed through the earth.

This talk reminded me of my hunger. After meeting Malka earlier, she'd put me off my breakfast. I didn't need much, but I was hungry. I couldn't help glancing at the rhythmic pulse in her neck. "The ground is full of information, as you will find out when you develop your earth skills."

"You sound serious and convincing, but it's unbelievable. I want to see proof."

Without commenting, I allowed my fangs to descend. Before I was able to flash my toothy smile, the sharp sound of rain pattering on glass distracted us, and we stared at the window together.

"I never expected rain. It wasn't on the forecast," she said.

"It is my guess that Fire is telling the Water Boy about you right now."

"What?" she asked while staring intently at her house.

I watched the droplets of water slide down the panes of glass in the sash windows. "It always rains when he is upset."

She wasn't listening. Why would she be interested when I was talking about a person she wasn't aware existed? All her attention focused on the house opposite and the front door as it opened.

The young man whom I had mentioned stepped forth.

There was no way my hungry fangs were going back into place with him in view. Oblivious to rain, Water Boy wore no top. He did not need to cover up his perfect swimmer's body. He was in excellent physical shape and showing it off to best advantage in mere lightweight baggy trousers.

After descending the steps from the front door, he paused on the pavement and held his hands up. The rain landed on his palms for a few seconds before he placed them against his cheeks in the way one might rinse one's face in a basin of water.

"How strange," Malka whispered as he turned his face up to the sky and ran his fingers through his hair.

I thought nothing of it though I understood interacting with the rain in that way might seem strange to someone unfamiliar with the ways of witches.

After basking in his element, Water Boy looked in our direction and walked toward us. He must have seen us sitting by the window. The rain cleared up just as suddenly as it had started. Again, no surprise.

Malka held her breath as she watched in fascination. I would have done the same if I breathed. He was breathtakingly beautiful, and he tasted that good too.

"He's coming this way," she whispered. With no concern for subtly, she leaned forward to get a better view as he commenced climbing the set of steps to my front door. When he disappeared out of sight, the bell rang, and I recognized Maria's footsteps as my female servant went for the door.

Malka turned to me and whispered, "Why do you think he's not wearing a top? Are you sure we've not died and gone to heaven? You know, hot guys with no shirts seems like my idea of heaven."

I laughed. "Water Boy isn't partial to clothing. I think it might please you to know that like oil repels water, he repels clothes at every opportunity."

"All his clothes?" she seemed to be thinking aloud.

I laughed. "You and I could be friends, Malka."

She looked at me and gasped.

I saw the shock on her face at the very second when she spotted my fangs.

She did ask to see them.

CHAPTER TEN

One hell of a toothy smile
Malka Selby

ARE THOSE TEETH REAL?

Did he put fake teeth in his mouth while a semi-naked man walked through the rain outside and distracted me? I wanted to see plastic joke teeth come away from his gums. I didn't know what to make of the possibility that they were real, and he'd been telling the truth. That I'd survived sinking into the earth like a woman with lead boots in a swimming pool and was sitting and talking with a vampire was no less credible than believing this was the afterlife.

At the sound of footsteps entering the room, I turned, expecting to see the shirtless man from outside, but a mature woman wearing a yellow floral apron over a dress stood before us.

"Sir." She curtseyed. "Beck Colborn is at the door."

"Show him in, Maria. Beck never needs to be left outside. And bring in some water."

The lady's gaze darted to me but didn't linger before dropping to the floor. Through eleven years in posh boarding schools, I'd visited many grand homes that had servants; however, Maria seemed incongruous in this average terraced London home. A please and thank you from Varu wouldn't go amiss, either. How hadn't I noticed Varu's arrogance from the start?

"She's wondering about you being here." He didn't wait for Maria to leave the room before speaking about her in a low voice. "She should know Beck's always welcome. He doesn't need an announcement."

With rain droplets glistening on his bare chest, the man entered. He appeared unselfconscious as he walked toward us. He stopped in the middle of the room and dropped his head into something that was more than a nod but not quite a full deferential bow.

I might not have noticed the subtle behavior but for having watched Maria curtsey beforehand. It left me wondering who the fuck I was sitting with. Who was this Varujan, the Romanian vampire who had servants and visitors bowing to him?

"Come on in, Beck. To what do I owe the pleasure?" Varu remained seated.

I stood up and held out my hand, dragging my eyes from Beck's tattooed torso and up to his face. I might be dead, or possibly not, but I hadn't forgotten my manners.

The stranger's smile was as sexy as his body, a little crooked and a lot cheeky. We held eye contact as Beck walked toward me, and then a big warm hand clasped mine.

"You're fully aware of how eager I am to meet Malka." Answering Varu, Beck's eyes never left my face. "I'm Beck Colborn, and I'm pleased to meet you at long last."

"And you didn't consider bothering with clothes?" Varu chuckled.

"I didn't stop to think about it." Beck glanced down at his body as if he had no idea what he was wearing. My gaze went with his. Raindrops clung to his broad shoulders, and one or two streamed down his body, cutting a curved path over the ridges of his stomach muscles.

The movement of his head forced me to look up. He grinned at me, having caught me staring at his body. I didn't want to stop at looking. I blushed. Our hands had been together for a little too long, so I let go and sat down.

No one in possession of their full faculties stepped out of their house, at night, in the rain, and didn't realize they were only wearing jogging bottoms and sneakers. I deduced Beck might be gorgeous, but he couldn't be the full ticket.

"I was in a hurry to get out of there."

"Fire in a bad mood?"

"Mmmm, yes, but more that I wanted to come and meet you, Malka. Once Haydn told me you were here, there was no keeping me away."

Beck pulled a chair away from the dining table and sat close to me. His knees spread wide apart; his feet rested on either side of me, so I was almost enveloped between his legs. Almost. He'd positioned himself just far enough from me for it not to feel too suffocatingly close, but near enough that it seemed we were embarking on a long-term relationship that might end in marriage.

His widely spread legs, of course, beckoned my gaze toward his crotch, but using great willpower, I resisted the urge to check out the goods presented to me.

Oh, for fuck's sake, my eyes swept over his entirety, as they did a sweep of the entire room. I didn't linger or stare, but I tried to memorize what I saw for later re-examination.

Despite the way he'd entered, I had the impression Beck was familiar enough with the inside of Varu's house to make himself at home and rearrange the furniture. He sighed and turned to Varu. "When Haydn came home, I was almost asleep. He woke me up. We argued."

Varu nodded. "He was annoyed when he left here."

"Why did you want to meet me in such a hurry?" I asked.

"I've heard so much about you from Air and Haydn."

"Air?" I echoed in bewilderment.

"Yes. And, naturally, I've always wondered what it will be like when you return."

"Naturally?" Echoing whatever he said became the way to converse. Beck seemed to miss that these weren't just words but questions.

He bit his lip and looked at Varu as if seeking help. The vampire's expression remained unchanged and impossible to read.

"And I'm here because Haydn told me you're in this house, and you didn't want to come home with him."

"Can you blame me? He's an ass. And he just attempted to murder some women right in front of me. For all we know, they are dead. And he behaves like it was all no big deal. How can I trust him not to take a swing at me?"

"Ha! He didn't make a wonderful impression then." Beck laughed, as if he wasn't one bit surprised about the poor first impression.

But who laughs when they are told their friend might have murdered two women? This cute guy was apparently a sandwich short of a full picnic.

"If I may explain, Malka, he didn't murder any women." Varu's trick teeth were no longer visible, and I hadn't seen him remove them.

"But I saw it happen."

"Did you see blood?"

"No, I didn't stop to check them for a pulse, either. But if they aren't dead, they were hurt, and they could have died."

"You wouldn't have found a pulse. He didn't kill them, because they were already dead. There was no blood because he cut down vampires, and they hadn't eaten." Varu crossed one leg over the other. "I don't know if he killed them or just injured them, but I can tell you, we don't have pulses."

He held up his arm, offering his wrist to me should I wish to check for a pulse.

I didn't.

"And they were threatening you. So, it wasn't quite a cold-blooded attack by Fire; it was self-defense. He was perfectly right to take such action."

I was surprised to hear Varu defend Haydn when they seemed at loggerheads over everything.

Beck cast a side-eyed glance at Varu. "Haydn's infuriating at times, but he wouldn't hurt anyone if he didn't have to." He winked and added, "And vampires don't exactly count as people in his eyes."

I turned to look at Varu. "If you really are a vampire, why aren't you bothered about their deaths?"

"I'm not in any way connected to the Turkish vampires. They're a modern group," he said dismissively. "Those vampires were unfamiliar to me, and I'm not sure if he ended their existence. Their heads were still attached when we left them."

'*Heads were still attached,*' was a phrase I didn't need to hear. "Aren't you worried Haydn will kill you?" I pressed.

Beck raised his eyebrows, and Varu shook his head. "He wouldn't. We have peace on this road."

"That's right. It's a peaceful road. And I've come here to see if there's any way I can tempt you over to our side of the street."

I turned my full attention to Beck once again. He was the third man I'd met this evening who lived on this street, and just like the others, he was certainly something beautiful to look at. Unfortunately, they were all as batshit crazy as characters from the Mad Hatter's tea party. "Well, I'll have to think about it."

"Take your time. As I said, I'm here to tempt you." His legs seemed to part a little wider, and his crotch raised a little. That was probably just in my crazy mind.

"Are you propositioning me?" He could tempt me into many things.

His chest expanded. I don't know about the other parts; I didn't look.

Seriously, I did *not* look.

"If you like."

I like, all right.

"Let's just get the flirting done with and get to the point." Varu shifted in his seat. "She's ready for the knowledge of you, Beck. I hate to disappoint you, Malka, but Water Boy won't give you everything you're hoping for. At least, not tonight. He'll make you wait."

My cheeks heated as I stumbled for a retort. "You've got it all wrong about me, after what I said about heaven and hot men earlier." I totally failed to find any witty comeback.

At that moment, Maria entered, carrying a tray with two glasses and a jug of water with slices of lemons and ice. This time she didn't curtsey, but she maintained her interest in the carpet. She put the tray on the dining table and backed out of the room.

Without acknowledging the interruption, Varu said, "I have a predator's sense of smell, Malka. When your body's aroused, it gives off the most delightful odor."

I was mortified. It was bad enough when dogs put their faces up against your crotch. "Are you saying you've been sniffing my damp panties while I'm wearing them?"

Beck snickered.

Varu shrugged. "Sorry. Can't help it." And I noticed those teeth again as he grinned.

I wasn't going to be outdone. I was a British queen of upping the ante, especially after it worked so well the night before.

"You're half wrong and half right about me wanting Beck in that way. I'd actually imagined a threesome with the two of you." I'd intended to shock them, but they both looked at me with smiling approval. If that didn't surprise them, if they liked the idea of a ménage à *trois* I could do one better. "And by that, I mean me watching you two fuck each other as well."

That got a reaction, but nothing that I might have expected. They glanced at each other, winked, and smiled right back at me—smirks on their smug faces.

"Wait!" Some of the things slotted into place. "Hold on. Are you two actual, real-life lovers?"

"I can't be real life anything, Malka. I'm not alive. As for lovers, well, it's complicated."

Varu and Beck exchanged glances.

"Not exactly." Beck shrugged. "You should tell her."

"When I picked Beck up in a gay club years ago, drinking his blood and fucking him was what I had in mind. It's an interminable story, but suffice to say things didn't work out that way."

"So far." Beck raised one shoulder, suggesting things might change in the future.

Fuck me sidewards.

These guys had totally turned my game on me. The next goal of my sex life was to watch two guys fucking. I wouldn't mind it being these two guys.

"Are you telling me that despite sniffing my panties all night, my fantasies about you and me are staying as just that because you're a gay vampire?" I knew gay and bi and trans people. It was no big deal. It was just unexpected, because I thought he'd been flirting with me. How had I misread the signals?

"That's not a simple question," he answered mysteriously.

"Hey, I didn't imagine it. You were coming on to me in the Smoothie Shack, not the other way around. Or were you just trying too hard to win customers with your charm? Or were you hoping to lure me somewhere and drink my blood?"

Beck put his hand on my knee. "If you're going to ask questions, you need to stop firing them at him and give Varu a chance to answer."

Okay, so Water Boy had my runaway pattern of speech all worked out already and was prepared to challenge me on it.

"Vampire desires aren't the same as for humans. And, since you ask, Malka, since the moment I met you, I've wanted to drink your blood. I still do. Blood is better than sex, for us, most of the time. Although nothing can beat the two things together."

“A vampire’s bite doesn’t have to kill you or turn you into a vampire, Malka,” Beck added. “It is amazing.” He seemed to go glassy-eyed and speak from experience.

“But I promised Fire that I wouldn’t bite you tonight,” Varu said.

“That arrogant prick, Haydn, is Fire?” I asked.

Varu nodded.

“He’s not the boss of me and gets no say what I do with my body or my blood, I’ll have you know.” I had a good mind to offer all my blood to Varu right then out of rebellious spite.

“He doesn’t. But I’ve made a promise to him that I consider binding for one night only. Now everything else will be easier for you to understand. Before Beck arrived, I was telling you the basics about witches and vampires, but Beck here would be better at filling you in.”

Hmmm, filling me in: that’s exactly what I imagined.

“Filling you in on the details of your kind. Witches, I mean. Not what you’re thinking.”

“Can you read minds?” I wondered if that was a vampire skill.

Beck laughed out loud, and from the corner of my eye, I thought his legs spread a little further, and his crotch bulged even more.

“No. That I can’t do that, but I can read you by your scent, Malka. I know a great deal about you.”

“He can smell everything. When you’re scared or when you’re turned on, your body chemistry changes, and you can’t hide it from him,” Beck explained. “Some witches also have that powerful sense of smell.”

Well, I couldn’t argue with the facts.

“Okay, so we’ve established I have sex on the brain. Varu will not touch me tonight. You two met in a gay club, and you’ve come over here with hardly any clothes on to tempt me. Tell me what I need to know. And one of those things has to be, are you gay or bi or what?” I needed to find out what Varu meant when he said Beck would make me wait.

Breathing in deeply, Beck's chest expanded and his shoulders went back.

And my undies got wetter.

And Varu probably knew about my undies. He might have been wondering if the chair I sat on was damp. And once I thought of it, I wondered the same thing.

"I'm not gay, Malka. I'm bisexual. And as we're being so honest, I like your fantasy about the three of us, but Varu's right. It can't happen today."

How frustratingly cryptic. "Why not? Look, I've just had a near-death experience, you gotta understand. I don't normally have threesomes with guys I've just met." I blushed, thinking about the previous night. As sequences of events go, it wasn't a bad idea. I wouldn't mind if some variations on the actions of the night before played out every single day for the rest of my life. With time off when I had my period. "I want to feel alive. I am still alive, aren't I?" I'd lost track of whether or not I was dead.

"You are very much alive," Varu confirmed.

"And I'm an earth witch? Is that true?"

"Yes," Beck said. "You're an earth witch."

"Haydn?"

Beck nodded. "Yes, he's a fire witch."

"So tell me how you fit in around here. I don't mean fit in. I just speak the language of double entendre fluently. I mean, just tell me more."

The huge manly figure settled into the chair as if preparing to tell a lengthy story. His reluctance to get on with it meant he probably didn't much like talking about himself. That alone was a good sign. I'd met enough men who wanted to talk at inordinate length about themselves.

"When I met Varu, I didn't understand I was a witch. He didn't kill me, as you can see. He brought me home, here, and we talked. He introduced me to Haydn, who took me in, and taught me about our kind and how to use my abilities."

"Varu calls you Water Boy, so I'm guessing you're a water witch?"

"That's right. I'm water, Haydn's fire, your mother is air, and now you've turned up, we can form an elemental coven." Beck stood up and walked to the table.

"Elemental coven?" I had to stop repeating what he said every few minutes. It was annoying me already.

"Yes. You know, earth, air, water, and fire. Do you want a drink?" He pointed at the jug of water.

There were only two glasses, and I assumed he was asking me, but I wasn't at all sure of the etiquette here. "Water? Yes, please. I'm sorry, Beck, but I don't have much idea of what you're talking about." That was a lie. I had *no* idea what he was talking about.

He cocked his head to one side and looked at me as if I were a curiosity. "Haydn warned me you haven't been raised in our world. I didn't presume you knew nothing." He casually pointed at the jug of water while still looking at me. Water from the pitcher floated into the air and poured itself into the two glasses as if it was siphoned through an invisible tube.

The only thing that stopped me from freaking out was that I'd freaked myself out of freak earlier in the evening. I was completely all out of freak. First, the ass across the road murdered people in front of my eyes. No, that was second because it was after he threw me out of the way of machete man. I died. I didn't die. I sat talking to a vampire, like a character out of an Anne Rice novel. Really, there was no single shred of freakability left in me.

I didn't remark on the magic, trick, illusion, whatever I'd just witnessed. Instead, I calmly said, "Let's start our conversation again and assume I *do* know nothing."

Varu stretched out his arms, his fangs still visible. I guess that was the vampire equivalent of letting your hair down when at home or lounging around in your PJs. “If it’s any help, I can tell you she definitely knows nothing,” he said.

His statement seemed a bit rude, but accurate. “I used to like him,” I grumbled.

Beck handed me a glass of water and then picked up the second for himself. “Of all the witches in the world, only a few are elementals. We’re more magical than most, and our powers are amplified when we work together. Your mom is an air witch, and there are plenty of air witches around. There are several on this street. Fire and water are less common, but we’re here.”

“What about earth witches? Are we common?”

Beck shook his head. “No, very rare.”

“Okay.” I wasn’t sure how to feel about being rare. Did it make me special or odd? Did I want to be rare and different? Did I have a choice?

“I’m the new guy around here. I never met your mother, and as far as I know, no one knows who your father was. You don’t have a functioning coven here because of your mother’s extended absence. Covens are always headed by a priestess, a female witch. She’s usually the most powerful witch in the coven. You’d be the obvious person to take over as High Priestess and reinstate the Summer House Coven. Haydn’s already sworn a sacred oath to you, so you’re pretty much bound together. Likewise for Air; they are sworn to protect you. So, you have three elements, guaranteed: fire, air, and earth. It’s just down to you and me to decide whether I join your elemental band. Well, completely up to you, to be honest. I get very little say in it.”

“Water Boy,” muttered Varu, who had great amusement written across his face.

I raised my hand. “Hold on. Back it up there. I don’t know anything about oaths that bind us for life, but I’m damn sure I’d not agree to be bound with flaming Haydn. And who is this air character? And are you saying the bottom line is I can turn up and chuck you out? God, you must hate me.” I did not like the sound of any of it.

Before she went on the killing spree that landed her in prison, my mom had obviously attracted these loonies and formed a pact with them while I was a child. Now, my mom was housed in a secure unit for the criminally insane, for a good reason and a ghastly murder.

"They," Varu interrupted. "Air are a they, and the three of them live two doors down from Haydn. Beck, you have to keep in mind that she's ignorant about the magical world. Your oaths, covens, and magic are all new to her."

"That's right," I agreed with Varu. "I've only just discovered I'm not dead, and that came as a shock. I'm a witch. And he's a vampire. And I'm not sure that last part is true or any of it. They look like false fangs to me." I jabbed a pointing finger in Varu's direction. "It's a lot to take in. And to believe I'm dead or dreaming in a coma seems a more likely explanation for this madness than the story you two are telling me. One thing I can tell you is this: there is no way I'm going to be bound to that ass from across the road."

"I don't like to tell you unwelcome news when we've only just met, but you are bound with Haydn by magic, whether or not you like it." Beck raked his fingers through his hair and sighed. "Believe me, since I met him, I've often wished he was free, but only your mother can break the spell. By the way, I don't hate you, but I have always been anxious about your return and what it will mean for me."

It was all a hell of a lot of information and responsibility to lay at my feet. I knew I was coming into wealth. I was days aware from accessing my trust fund on my twenty-first birthday, and with riches comes responsibility. But this was too much.

"What does that mean? This bond, you make it sound like marriage?" I glanced at Varu, but his poker face gave nothing away, and he patiently waited for Beck to explain.

"No, it's not a marriage. It's not romantic unless you want it to be. He is sworn to protect you and be a part of your life. If you join a new coven or move away, he will follow you." Beck took a sip of his water. "He'll support you forever."

"But I've lived away since I was seven, and he's stayed here."

"Yes, that's right. He stayed in your house; he looked after your financial affairs. And Air went with you to watch over your personal well-being."

"Air?" No, I wasn't going to keep repeating his words. "Air has been following me?" That sounded like the talk of a madwoman. I was officially becoming my mother.

Varu leaned toward me. "Air are three witches, and they've been with you wherever you've been these last few years. They were there to keep a watchful eye on you in case you got into trouble or if your abilities emerged earlier than usual. You will have seen them without knowing they are witches from Stoke Newington."

"That's right," Beck agreed. "We all felt sure you'd come back here ahead of your twenty-first birthday. Air contacted us last night when you arrived in London. One of them came here. They also told us you stumbled across hell hounds last night by chance. Today, Haydn went out looking for you to make sure you arrived here safely, even though Tuuli and Niall were out there."

"Tuuli and Niall?" I was still doing it.

"They're two of the three air witches, Chet's the third. All three of them are in the third house along the street right now. It's one of the houses we usually let out to rent."

"Pardon?"

"We might be witches, and your family owns lots of property, but we still have to eat and pay bills. Renting the houses out to tenants has been the best way to cover running costs."

"Okay, that sounds reasonable. It's just it brings a new meaning to the term Airbnb." Even I wasn't sure if I'd made a joke. None of us laughed.

Neither Varu nor Beck spoke for a moment. Varu stood up, walked around the table, and paced at the far end of the room, which wasn't far away at all.

Watching him move drew my gaze to the dark wooden display unit behind him that housed many colorful ornaments, plates, diminutive boxes, and pieces of china. The cabinet itself was nothing special to look at, but it appeared old, sturdy, and as if had withstood a fair old battering. The house was modest, given all he'd told me and what I'd seen below ground.

"Okay, I'm more confused than ever, and I might be getting a headache."

Varu stopped pacing. "Congratulations, Beck. You've turned her off." He tapped the side of his nose. His focus moved between Beck and me and then lingered on some distant place outside the window before he resumed pacing.

If he itched to get some air, I understood how he felt. They had bombarded me with bizarre information in a short time since entering this room, and I longed to get out of it.

"Beck?" I prompted. "I thought you were explaining why we couldn't have a threesome, which better not be because I'm promised by magic to asshole Haydn."

The shirtless man sat up a little straighter. "I was getting to it. Elemental witches are few in number and more powerful than other witches. If we work together, we can harness the combined power of the magical elements to bring about harmony. That's what witches do, by the way—maintaining the balance in nature is our mantra, our raison d' être. The ideal is to create a coven of different elementals and use the most powerful way to channel our combined magic."

"That makes sense," I said.

"Malka, he's talking about sex magic." Varu stopped walking and leaned forward over the table.

"Oh." I hadn't realized that.

"Sex is the best way for elemental witches to make spells or whatever it is you do. So Beck won't just give in to the urge to do what he wants with you or me because he wants to save his energies for magic." The most surprising thing about what Varu said was the way he said it, as if he really cared. Varu was obviously fond of Beck, and I sensed there was more they hadn't told me. I didn't possess the full story.

CHAPTER ELEVEN

The territory of the lone Romanian elder
Varu Vasile

THE WHISPERING, SCRATCHING, and scraping at a pitch that humans couldn't hear pulled the focus of my senses away from the amusing delights within my house. I would never have survived so long if I'd ignored my enemies when they gathered at the very edge of my territory.

"You two witches have much to discuss, and you don't need me for the conversation. I will leave you for a while."

"Are you going out to eat?" The longing look in his eyes begged me to stay and drink from him. Water Boy bewitched me in a way I hadn't known in decades. I didn't know why Beck got under my skin in a way that very few people did.

With Malka's innocent, curious eyes gazing at me, I didn't think it appropriate to discuss my dining habits. Finding out about witches was probably enough for one night.

"Malka is staying here as my guest tonight. You know your way around my house, Beck. Please, show her where she can get cleaned up and sleep."

I didn't want to leave them. On the contrary, I wanted to stay with them both and satisfy my hunger.

My younger self would have struggled to resist fucking the girl who wanted it so badly. The delicious perfume of her arousal affected me greatly. In order to fuck her, I'd need to feed, and I longed to taste her forbidden blood and feel its nourishing power inside me.

The sweet-smelling virgin boy would have gladly offered to feed me, as he had done many times before. The blood of a virgin elemental was usually more tempting than sex, and for several years Beck had provided me with the very best sustenance.

Ideally, in my daydreams, I'd bask in the combined fluids of both of these dangerous, powerful witches.

All my senses, the incredible hearing, and the enhanced sense of smell and sight warned me that the nearby threat was real and growing.

Stepping toward the hallway, I bade them farewell. "Call Maria if you need anything. She'll do your bidding, Beck." I rarely trusted a witch in my home and in command of my servants; there had been none since Malka's parents.

Before exiting, I stood at my threshold to compose myself, ready for battle. It was at a time like this that, if I were human, I would take a few deep breaths. Instead, I emptied my mind for several seconds to ready myself. I opened the door but didn't step out onto the street. I set my senses on a preliminary reconnaissance mission.

The fragrant herbs and spices hit me first: the essence of tomatoes and the dough of the lahmacun that the people ate before they fed these vampires. It was as if I ate it fresh from the oven. They were all of Turkish origin, the vampires and their food, and their food's food.

Too late, I realized that I should have drunk what Water Boy wanted to give me. These vampires would sense my hunger just as I smelt their food.

They considered hunger a sign of weakness, even though it could be a matter of choice. It was a strength that we vampires didn't have to feed.

On the other hand, if I'd approached them with the scent of elemental blood fresh on my fangs, it would have been an impressive show of strength. Few vampires had the opportunity to drink from elementals. I had drunk from many over the years.

There was little more prized than their blood, especially when willingly given.

There would have been no better way of showing the enemy that the witches and the sole vampire of Summer House Road were united in solidarity.

As soon as I stepped out of the door, I saw them at the end of the street, fifteen of them. They were all young. We all *looked* young; we didn't age. But those vampires *were* young.

The thin slither of enchanted rock salt embedded into the road by the witches was almost imperceptible to the naked human eye, but its powerful charm prevented vampires and other undesirable creatures from crossing and progressing into Summer House Road from this direction.

To gain entry from the other end, they'd have to cross Abney Park Cemetery first, which was my territory. Very few of our kind would take that route without my prior permission when trespassing can be a capital offense.

I walked to the very edge of the enchanted barrier and stopped on my side. I couldn't cross it. This was not my route away from my home.

Some young, overweight punk with blue hair sidled up to stand in front of me. "Vampire. You're on the wrong side of the line."

"I'm on my property so, frankly, I don't understand what you're talking about."

"We lost blood today. That can't be allowed to happen."

"You are right. It can't." At least we were in agreement. "We must preserve the local truce. Did someone die?"

"Damla died. It wasn't instant, but it was fast and painful. She experienced every second of the silver's toxic journey through her system. Ceyhan survives so far, but she's very ill and in great pain too. There was more than pure silver to his knives. The ginger witch who attacked our kin set out armed to murder, and he's still on the Abney estate. You need to hand him over for justice."

But Fire is a formidable enemy.

Trained from childhood as a vampire hunter, by the age of eleven he was an accomplished killer. He knew more about our kind than most witches and many vampires.

Slaying the undead is challenging; we don't die easily and quickly recover from minor injuries.

Given the right weapons, made of silver and laced with magic, he had the knowledge and skill to bring about a swift death or a slow and painful one. And he was never unarmed. By wielding nothing other than his fire element he could quickly reduce a small army of vampires to ash.

We don't recover from that.

Never underestimate Fire.

"You go out armed for murder so long as you have your teeth, young man. I don't know you, so I'm guessing you are unfamiliar with me," I said. "I see no sign of Abdil here. He is still your leader, isn't he?"

What I saw was a group of Turkish youth all done up similar to those we'd seen earlier. They wore scruffy black clothes and excessive face make-up, both the girls and the boys. They looked like modern, stereotypical vampires, but I also recognized it as contemporary youth fashion.

And then there were also the English kids—no, not just English, human. A few were relaxed and having fun and obviously had no idea that they accompanied vampires or what was happening here. I'd have to monitor those kids because they might step over the magical barrier as if it were simple table salt. To them, it was.

And a small group of people caught my attention. I barely glanced at them. It wasn't the sight of them I noticed; it was their rare and delightful scent—human adult virgins.

Even in all my undead years, I hadn't discovered why human blood changes its composition when they lose their virginity. It is not a change that takes place after any kind of sex, and not after masturbation, only after they've had penetrative sex. The blood of adult virgins tasted distinctive, and it reeked a wholesome calling card.

These young vampires in front of me must have been well-fed to resist such a delicious temptation. Or they had been forbidden to touch those three virgins under threat of a harsh penalty.

"You're the lone Romanian. We don't need Abdil's permission to deal with local crimes like the slaughter of our family."

I pursed my lips as I contemplated my best approach when faced with such nonsense. "The injury of your young Turkish vampires would have been avoided if they'd kept to the local code. The witch acted in self-defense. Furthermore, young man, the incident did not take place on your territory, but on mine. And, I should not need to add a warning about picking your friends and enemies carefully, but I will. You do not want to pick enemies among the residents of Summer House Road."

The impudent vampire laughed in my face. "I'll pick my friends, all right."

I hadn't met with such contemptible rudeness since a run-in with a bunch of racist skinheads years earlier. They didn't last long. Their names live on as the victims in one of the great unsolved murder cases of the 1970s.

Sadly, I couldn't deal with insolent young vampires as I dealt with humans. I didn't want to start a feud with my vampire neighbors. It was bad enough that the thousand-year war with witches continued, despite the local truce.

Apart from anything else, these youths had numbers on their side, and their territory surrounded mine. I could survive without leaving my land for years, but no one wants to live under siege.

"Kyle, stand down." An elegant vampire of considerable maturity approached. She had long black hair, and while her face appeared youthful, her demeanor and dress made it obvious she had been a vampire for decades.

The blue-haired vampire turned—apparently his name was Kyle, which didn't sound very Turkish. It more or less confirmed what I already knew. Kyle was young, recently turned, and British born.

He took several steps back but continued to watch me.

"Damla and Ceyhan are his cousins. Or were. We don't know if Ceyhan will live. We've brought a peace offering for you, Varujan." The lady who stepped up beside Kyle knew my name, at least. "Not one, but three English virgins of maturity are here for you. You can turn them, feed on them, or kill them. No penalties." She cast a glance in the direction of the three I'd noticed earlier.

Feigning disinterest, I didn't follow her gaze. My act would have fooled no one; my hunger was palpable. I wished I'd eaten earlier. If I were human, my empty stomach would be rumbling and my mouth salivating.

"From what I've heard, you might want to turn them, so you have some like-minded company. Is it true that you only see humans and witches these days?"

I screwed my face up as if I were thinking about her question. In fact, I was taking stock of the scene across the salt line.

Kyle moved away to talk to other vampires. His senses remained alert, however, focused on the virgins. There was tension over that side of the salt line, and I wondered about a pack of vampires holding onto so much potent blood, keeping it within hands reach and yet forbidden to drink from it.

There's a reason vampires are more often solitary, in my experience. We don't share well. We don't like rules. We don't like self-restraint, at least, not when it is imposed on us.

"When did you last have a vampire visit you?" she probed. "Your parties of yesteryear are famous."

I didn't know this young lady, but she knew more about me than I would have liked, and her words stabbed cruelly at the heart of my pain. Knowledge was power. And I had no clue what was so important that warranted a bribe of human virgins.

Vampire feeding was a free for all so long as we didn't kill our humans. We'd compel them and clear their memories. Regrettably, killing them was prohibited, and an essential part of the truce.

As for turning them, there were rules and customs about creating new vampires. Rules among vampires and rules agreed with witches brought about some temporary reprieve from the ongoing war between us.

"Do they know they are being offered as a sacrifice?"

She chuckled. "What do you think?"

"Their heartbeats are calm and steady. From their odor, I'd say they do not understand the danger of the vampires surrounding them."

The woman smirked.

"To consume humans until death or turn them into one of us at will are both outlawed. Have you cleared the gift with the Supreme High Priestess?"

Nodding, she gave a knowing smile. "They saw the tall witch with the flaming hair cutting down vampires. There are many witnesses. He went out armed and ready to attack and kill us. He broke the code. We're entitled to punish him. However, I heard he's a friend of yours. If so, we will take that into account if you wish. We can grant clemency to the friend of a vampire elder."

"You have heard wrong. We are not friends, merely neighbors due to a quirk of history when I assumed ownership of one side of the street and a witch took over the other side. Today, he'll take in a parcel for me if I'm sleeping. I'll water his plants if he goes away."

"And your territory is protected by his magic." She looked down at the ground. "When he went nuclear, he dropped his guard for a second, it was enough for everyone to see your neighbor is no lowly male. He's a powerful elemental. And his blood might save poor Ceyhan."

"It would seem that way. A quirk of history, however. I am sure the witches laid this magic to protect their home and not mine. We live on the same street, which is on the same historic patch of ground and, therefore, within my territory."

"If you have to choose, would you help one of your own, poor dying Ceyhan, or a witch?"

"I am not familiar with Ceyhan, and I have seen hundreds of vampires die over my lifetime, many at the hands of vampire hunters. One more deceased vampire makes no difference to me." I sounded like a callous loner, devoid of caring. That was how this female saw me, so she didn't question what I said. "The same is true for witches. I care not whether they live or die."

"If you have no care for witches, you will have no trouble in helping us. We will see him punished. We will be happy to take the new girl away instead of him. She's of no consequence to you, is that right?"

"There are several girls in this street, but if you are talking about the girl I accompanied in the cemetery, she is my houseguest and under my protection."

The lady shook her head. "She is an earth elemental. She must be presented to the Supreme High Priestess. The Council has charged me with this task."

"Really? We do not serve the witches' council. Is Abdil aware of your cooperation with our enemies?"

"Let me introduce myself, Varujan. I'm Cynthia Ward, Abdil's sponsored protégé. I've been communicating directly with the Supreme High Priestess on his behalf. The matter of the new elemental has been a priority since it became known that one was at large. We've done a deal to deliver the earth witch to the Priestess."

"And do you mind telling me since when you've become aware of this earth elemental?"

The lady smiled. "The witches have known for some time that something was afoot. There were prophecies, and premonitions; their oracles had visions. In recent years as she came into power, there were tremors across the world; many made international news. The witches couldn't identify the young witch because she kept moving. They still wouldn't be able to find her without our help, not just yet. You know our senses, Varujan. We see her aura. We saw the most powerful witch alive get off a bus in East London today."

"The girl has a big aura." No need not to state the fact. I smiled back at Cynthia Ward. "You might be after the wrong lady. I've no reason to believe the girl in my house is an earth."

"You will not make me doubt myself so easily." Cynthia shook her head and tapped her fingers over her lips. "No. You didn't take her through the earth. Don't take me for a fool. Once she used her magic, it confirmed the powerful witch with the big aura and the elemental that we sought were one and the same."

"Did you tell this to anyone?" A powerful earth witch in the house of Selby would shake things up for their hierarchy. The Supreme Council of Witches would see Malka as an emerging threat. However, as of yet, only vampires and demons could sense the power of her aura.

Cynthia laughed. "I have already dispatched a messenger to the Supreme Council of Witches to tell them the location of the unidentified earth elemental." Lowering her tone and assuming a more thoughtful expression, she continued, "No vampire from my clan would volunteer information to the witches. They won't learn from us that the girl is seventh order. I sense the highest order of power in her, do you?"

That the Supreme High Priestess knew of an earth witch in London was grim news, indeed. It could only have been more ominous if she knew Malka's potential. A seventh-order power would challenge the status quo, bringing chaos. Lack of clear leadership among the witches' council was only likely to lead to renewed attacks on vampires. But the young girl in my house could be most influential in years to come.

"What do you think will happen if the council gets their hands on a powerful earth witch?" I asked.

"We do deals with the council, but we don't help them. We will give them the elemental without telling of her potential. If we deliver her, it will cement our peace. It has been many years since we last had vampire hunters decapitating us in our sleep."

"Twenty-one years, that's all. It's the blink of an eye and fresh in my memory, as it will also be in theirs."

Twenty-one years since he died, murdered by a junior vampire hunter, a mere child.

She studied my face. "Is that when it happened? I recall it, and I'm sorry for your loss."

A successful vampire life is long and full of loss.

"If we deliver such a potent witch to them, they might use her as a weapon against us," I suggested.

"They might." She shrugged and looked around at her clan. In a hushed voice, she said, "Honestly, if they decide she is a threat to them, they will try to control her and eliminate her. That will happen once they find out about her abilities, but that could be years from now. The Priestess and her ilk are still our enemies, Varujan. When we deliver the girl, we'll be planting a living time bomb in their midst."

I sighed. "If you deliver a powerful earth elemental to them, you assist the council of witches. The earth witch will make them stronger."

Cynthia cocked her head to one side. I couldn't believe she hadn't already considered this. "Are you suggesting we eliminate the girl before she can cause any trouble? I like the thought of trouble for them, but not for us. We can say she put up a fight and was killed by accident. They need never be told about her seventh order abilities."

"Absolutely not. You will not use my houseguest as a pawn for your doomed experiment. I deny you access to my territory, so you cannot take her."

Cynthia's mouth fell open in surprise, and she dropped her gaze to the floor, focusing where the magical wall divided us. "From this direction, the magic denies us access. From the other direction, through Abney Park, we can enter your street. I hope you will grant us passage, as we do not want to trespass on a vampire elder. We're not your enemy."

The implications of trespassing on a vampire's property could mean death. She paused, choosing her words carefully.

"If we don't take her, others will come who can. Don't go to war with us, Varujan. Those witches in your street might not intend you harm, but when witches are at war with vampires, we must pick sides. All die equally under their silver blades, and you have little defense against them in the daytime."

I shook my head. "The girl might become our ally. Have you considered that?"

"If she lives, anything other than taking her to the High Priestess is not an option. Let's say we sleep on it and reconvene. I'll give you forty-eight hours to come to your senses and deliver the girl to us. If you do that, we'll forget about your red-headed friend. If you don't help us, we will come for both of them. We must take the girl. She's non-negotiable."

"Forty-eight hours," I repeated as I turned my back on the vampires.

I could do a little to help the elementals at night and nothing in the day, but if I chose to support the witches, I risked the relationship with my neighbors.

If I alerted Fire to the danger, none of the elementals would leave the safety of the salt circle, which magically protected their home. They'd survive a long time in Summer House Road under siege, but their charms wouldn't be enough to keep everyone out forever.

Humans can walk into protected areas with no awareness of the magic that stops vampires and demons.

"You can choose peace, push the earth girl across the line, and accept three virgins for your trouble. Or don't do any of that. We will find a different way to take her, and it might get messy."

There were times when I wondered if a continued alliance with the house of Selby was in my interest, and this was one of them.

CHAPTER TWELVE

Is it a room? Is it a cave? Is it a basement in Stoke Newington?
Malka Selby

WALKING DOWN THE TWELVE-million-step staircase was a lot easier than climbing it.

Although I wasn't looking forward to having to ascend yet again, Beck assured me we weren't going all the way to the bottom.

We'd reached sub-basement level, and I was kicking up an excellent speed going down when Beck stopped me.

"Do you want to see where the vampire sleeps?"

Who would say no to such a question?

Not me.

Beck pushed open a door, but neither of us stepped inside. You didn't just wander into someone's bedroom uninvited at the best of times. And of all bedrooms, this looked uninviting.

It was dark. There were no windows and no curtains. There was no furniture at all.

Freshly plowed bare earth substituted for a carpet.

The walls and ceiling comprised nothing more than dirt. The vampire cave was literally that. A bare hollow dug into the ground.

"Unbelievable. He really sleeps in there?"

"Yes, I know, right? You would think someone so old and wealthy would sleep in something big and grand. Although it is Romanian soil that he's shipped over especially to scatter on the floor."

More than the fangs, this was convincing evidence that our host was the blood-sucking demon he claimed to be. No sane person would have a room like that if they could afford wallpaper.

Beck placed a hand high on the doorframe and leaned against it. "I find, if you get too fond of him, it helps to remember where he sleeps. He's not a living human in the way that we are, albeit we're a magical subset of humans. This is where he sleeps, in this dirty little hole. I don't think any less of him for it. But it's a reminder that even though he looks like us, and he's extremely thoughtful and kind, he is a different species."

"He's a nocturnal blood drinker. That's not something I'd easily forget. What about you, are you too fond of him?"

"No danger of that. He pushes me back to Haydn all too often. Like we've already told you, Varu and I are just friends."

As we stood looking in the doorway, I noted the strange turn of phrase about a man who was supposedly saving himself: *Pushes me back to Haydn.* Beck might have meant the way Haydn trained him to be a witch, but I got the feeling there was more to it. Something distracted me before I could pry further.

Out of the corner of my eye, I noticed figures. I grabbed hold of Beck's arm, not knowing whether or not to be alarmed by the sight of Maria and a man watching us. "Should we be here?"

He saw them too. "We're fine at the moment, because Varu's not in there. They protect him when he's sleeping. Vampires are deadly when awake, almost impossible for a witch to beat in a fight without powerful magic, but vulnerable when they're asleep." Beck closed the door, and we set off down more stairs.

I didn't want to think about how Maria and the man might protect Varu if we'd intended him harm.

"Why does he trust you?" I asked.

"I don't honestly know. Vampires have abilities we don't. They see our auras. I must have a trustworthy one." Beck chuckled to himself. He paused on the next half-landing, where we'd do a complete turnabout.

"It isn't uncommon for witches and vampires to reach a mutually beneficial agreement for help and protection. That's what's going on here. I didn't know it then, but I was fortunate that Varu found me and brought me into a witching community when he did."

"But I don't understand. He mentioned vampires and witches are at war."

"There's never been a formal settlement to the conflict, so it is ongoing. But in reality, around here we're at peace. The war is out there, in a faraway sense." Beck flipped his hand out in front of him. "It's an important thing. There are local truces in most places, as far as I know. We aren't fighting in the streets with vampires each night or hunting them down and killing them where they sleep in the daytime."

We descended further.

What I saw earlier indicated the war was very much happening on the streets of Stoke Newington. But my head swam with all the fresh information. I couldn't do any more questions and answers. "I want to know much more, but I just need to clean up."

"We're there. You can clean up and relax in here."

Immediately below Varu's room, Beck pushed open a door, beyond which I hoped to see a traditional bedroom with an en-suite bathroom and not another hole in the ground.

My mouth fell open. I had not expected a cave.

"This is a very special place, in that few people have seen it."

"It's beautiful." It wasn't so much a cave as an underground garden. Despite the lack of daylight, a few plants flourished, but most of the beauty came from the stone sculptures, colorful rocks, and shiny gems all surrounding an underground pool. The water entered the room at a high level and curved over the edge of a rock, creating a short waterfall into the pool.

Many tiny white lights hung on strings of cable across the ceiling and twinkled like stars. Ropes of colorful little lights hung about the room, creating an atmosphere, energy, and moving shadows as light bounced across the surface of the water.

"Is it okay for you to bring me here? It's so private and, I was going to say, magical?"

Beck smiled. "It is magical, isn't it? I'm not a mind reader, but I just knew that Varu wanted you to bathe here. The water's maintained at a pleasant temperature."

"Water everywhere, but is there any to drink?"

"You can bathe in it and drink it perfectly safely. If you'd like chilled water, however, I can get you some from the fridge."

He pointed to a fridge in the corner of the room.

"Are you ready?"

I wasn't sure what he was asking or expecting, but I was ready to get in that water, so I said, "Yes."

That was when I discovered I wasn't prepared at all. He kicked off his footwear and bent over to pull down his jogging bottoms. I didn't see how good he looked in underwear because whatever he was wearing was all discarded in one seamless movement, socks and all.

Of course, when he bent over, my gaze went down with him, and when he stood back up, my pupils didn't move from the place where they'd fixed in surprise.

For several seconds I stared where I shouldn't; even in its flaccid state, it appeared long and thick. It dawned on me that I shouldn't be staring at or thinking about this man's cock. My head shot back up to face his face.

He winked at me. "Everything all right?" His voice was more of a deep rumble than previously.

"Fine," I squeaked. "I didn't realize we were getting in together."

I debated the wisdom of stripping naked to go skinny-dipping with a man I'd met less than an hour earlier. A man who claimed he was a witch. And I was in a secluded place where no one would hear me scream.

As I thought about it, he turned and slipped into the water. Even though he was a hunk to look at, he'd taken off his clothes in front of me with no sense of it being sexual, weird, or creepy. Upstairs, Varu and Beck had implied Beck was an untouched virgin who was saving himself, which all seemed hard to believe. Yet I didn't feel like he'd do anything uninvited.

I watched him swim, every muscle perfectly toned and accentuated by the magnification effect of the water. At this point, it's worth mentioning that it wasn't a cloudy lake; the water was crystal clear.

It didn't take me many seconds to decide on my best course of action.

It took a little longer for me to undress with my back turned to Beck and the water. I had no secret exhibitionist fantasies. No need to flash him my all, even if I didn't mind getting an eyeful of him. When I was nude, and turned to face the water, Beck was standing in the pool up to his chest with the waterfall cascading over his head and shoulders.

He called out as if I wasn't completely naked, "Come in, the water's perfect."

So is the view.

Perhaps I had died and gone to heaven after all.

It was more like a small lake than a large bath, so we had plenty of space. I could've swum laps. There was clearly a shallow end with steps, so I took that route and walked into the water. It was, as he described, the perfect temperature, and I enjoyed dipping my head under.

Just as I wondered about shampoo and soap, and then about towels, Beck called me. "Come here, under the waterfall so that I can wash your hair."

I swam over to him with no concern about our nudity. Once in the water, it seemed natural, especially as he was so at ease with the situation.

When I moved closer, various colorful bottles on a shelf cut into the rock and obscured by the flowing water came into view.

"The extract of lavender in this shampoo will help you relax." He squeezed a dollop of the mauve gel onto his palm. "I can see you've had a tough day. Turn around and let me wash your hair."

If washing hair was the talent of the water elemental, I wasn't about to complain. The fingers massaged my soapy scalp, working magic. In the tranquil surroundings, I relaxed and noticed just how tired I felt. The stress and excitement of the events of the day had left me drained.

"Witches have harnessed the soothing and healing properties of herbs and flowers for centuries," Beck explained, and even his voice sounded calm in my head. Despite his big muscular appearance, his touch was gentle and soothing—a contrast to many of the sadistic hairdressers who'd tortured me in the past.

Beck's fingers didn't stop on my head. The firm massaging fingertips worked their way down my neck. The tension left my shoulders and washed away in the water with the suds.

"The recipes for many health tonics and lotions aren't secret. Witches shared them with mankind. And we still use them today," he went on explaining, and I only half-listened. "It's like the healing power of touch. It's simple. Witches who aren't elementals use the same magic but without as much force behind it."

I leaned back against him, my head on his chest, my back against his stomach. For some reason, I let him continue to wash me. His hands ran a soapy, sweet-scented lather along my arms. The most intimate touch came when his fingers slotted in between mine.

I barely noticed the change as the soft cock that had been bobbing about in the water became harder as it brushed against my rear. I liked the sensation of it against me, so I moved my weight slightly from foot to foot so that I'd feel his cock rubbing against my back. It was all gentle but deliberate on my part.

"Is there anywhere else you'd like my fingers to help you relax?"

"What can a lady say to such a leading question? That's a hard one."

He didn't fall for my play on words.

"Why not just tell me the truth? My hands are ready to relax you all over in any way. Do you want me to?" He had me helpless before him, and I loved it. I loved his approach. I'd never had a man bathe with me and wash me before, and yet I believed Beck would have been content to do only that and nothing more. The man didn't seem the type to push things further if I said no. In fact, I doubted he'd make a move at all, so it was down to me to make things happen.

"You've done such a wonderful job on my head and shoulders, I'd like to find out what you'd do with other parts of me. But when we talked upstairs, you led me to believe you were saving yourself."

It was so difficult to believe what he told me. Beck had not said specifically, but implied he was a virgin who was saving himself, but not for his one true love. His virginity was needed for powerful magic. Apparently, the first time for an elemental virgin allowed great magic to be done.

I didn't have the heart to tell him that the V-boat had long since sailed for me.

Pushing back against him, I writhed, enjoying the sensation of his hard dick against the small of my back. I raised my arms and reached behind me with my hands to find his. Our fingers weaved together, and then I drew his hands forward to cover my breasts. He squeezed them and rolled the nipples between his fingers, making me moan.

"There are plenty of things I can do to you to make you feel good."

I didn't doubt it. As if he had a natural affinity with my body, Beck had the perfect touch.

Earth and water might not mix, if that was what we were, but it seemed we rubbed together pretty well as I melted under his liquid magic.

His hands on my breasts, his erection against my back, his lips on my neck had me moaning with pleasure.

When the attention to my breasts was no longer enough, one of his hands smoothed over my stomach, moving to find my private place where the wetness had a different viscosity from the surrounding pool.

"Very nice," he purred in my ear when a finger wiped over my swollen lady parts.

"You're telling me." If he enjoyed stroking me there as much as I liked the sensation, then this was a partnership that would work out well.

My legs opened a little wider, and I sank lower down in the water by just a couple of inches.

His fingers moved right under me so that his palm slid over my hard clit, and two or three fingers rested against my entrance.

We didn't need to drag out the foreplay. I was more than ready to receive his full thick length I had felt behind me. I wanted it. Water moved in channels through the earth, and I longed to experience him filling me and moving inside me.

"Maybe we should..." *Find a magical underwater condom?*

"Shall we get out of the water and enjoy this on dry land?" the water witch suggested. I was sure he'd be just as magical out of the water, so I didn't hesitate to agree.

Unfortunately, he withdrew his fingers but wrapped an arm around my shoulder and the other around my legs. He carried me the scant distance to the edge of the pool, where he lifted me onto the side.

The beauty of a magical underground garden was that the air temperature was warm, and there was no chilling breeze. I couldn't see any form of heating, but there must have been something warming the room and the water. The surrounding lights seemed to radiate heat.

"Are there any towels?"

He answered with a movement of his eyes, indicating they were, in fact, piled up and near at hand. I reached out and grabbed one. The cleverly designed room made the most of the naturally beautiful features and concealed its functional assets such as the shelf for toiletries and the stack of towels. The room contained everything one needed, tucked away but within easy reach, like magic.

"Make yourself comfortable."

I did. I lay back against the rock with my feet hanging over the edge into the water and my knees wide apart.

Beck stayed in the water, standing between my legs. We held eye contact beyond any comfortable period of time before he bowed down before me to introduce his tongue to my clit. At the same time, his fingers slipped inside to discover I was incredibly wet. They moved in easily.

His long fingers curled inside me in a perfect motion. As he drew them out, his thumb swept over my labia and clit. I didn't need more attention, but I welcomed it anyway. With perfect timing, his fingers plunged into my body again, and he repeated the action over and over with slight variations, an extra twist, a different speed, greater depth.

Each movement took me closer to a climax with his tongue and thumb, taking turns at my labia and the most sensitive nub.

He groaned. "Goddess, you taste so good." And his words reverberated against my pussy.

I spread my legs wide, wanting to give easy access.

His mouth took control over my private parts, licking and sucking at the area with such sexy enthusiasm.

Nice guys let women go first. When it came to sex, I'd met too many guys whose priority was what I might do for them. Beck's full focus was on what he could do for me as if that was how he'd derive his pleasure. If that was the case, and if he were a typical water elemental, I'd seek out water witches in the future.

My tunnel became fuller. He must've inserted another finger, and I wished my feet were on solid ground at this point so I could raise up and thrust my pussy in his face, but as my feet dangled in the water, I was helpless.

Unable to hold back the orgasm as it washed over me and through me like a wave, I could do nothing but come. My entire body pulsed, vibrating and shaking, as a tsunami of heat and emotion flooded through me. I couldn't have been wetter if he'd injected lubricant into me.

His fingers pounded faster, in time to the telltale sound of squelching. Generally, with a total stranger, I might have been embarrassed by that noise. Today, being so wet just seemed so hot, and Beck seemed to like it too.

Of the two of us, I wasn't sure who enjoyed it the most.

"Oh, God," he moaned. "You're incredible."

"Funny you should say that, as I was just thinking the same." I was putty in his hands, or as he had water magic, perhaps I melted into a liquid form. I'd never felt as aware of the wetness coming from me.

In quick succession, I came again and again. Each time I became less exhausted and more aroused. I had several orgasms in that same position, I'd turned into one big climactic mush at the mercy of his mouth and fingers.

I didn't know how this related to sex magic, but it was a fucking magical revelation to me.

He kissed my thighs while I recovered physically and identified feelings that I didn't recognize and didn't think were possible when having sex with a complete stranger. There was a connection between us—I wasn't sure if it was emotional or magical. I didn't understand it. Perhaps I was dead after all, and this was typical of sex in the afterlife. Or maybe the difference was to do with being in the home of a vampire.

"Perhaps you'd like to get out of the water so I could do something for you?" I asked when I'd caught my breath.

"You've done enough for me." He licked his lips and grinned.

"I'd really like you to fuck me." It was an impulse. The words slipped into my mind and out of my mouth without thinking. With him bringing me to orgasm in this way, I didn't understand the meaning of saving himself for magic.

Beck smiled at me and resumed kissing my thighs.

Perhaps I misunderstood the saving himself and virgin comments, as right now, it didn't seem possible.

Me being me, I couldn't stop myself speaking my thoughts: "I wonder if I'll be around when you need to do that big sex magic. I can't help wondering what position you'd fuck in to do magic. On my knees would be great. Do you use condoms for sex magic?"

With his mouth and hands busy, he didn't reply, but his eyes continued to smile.

"Say, are there condoms somewhere down here, hidden behind a rock?" This place seemed well equipped for anything. I glanced about casually until my gaze settled on the other man in the room, and my body temperature shot up with embarrassment. I wasn't an exhibitionist.

"I am sorry to disappoint you, but there are no condoms down here unless you've brought them yourself," Varu said.

CHAPTER THIRTEEN

V*ampires need blood if they are going to perform at their best*
Varu Vasile

MY FANGS DESCENDED automatically in response to the delightful scene of Malka and Beck driving each other wild. It was a feast for my hungry senses and the perfect antidote to my stomach-churning encounter at the southern perimeter of my territory.

Undetected, I entered the bathroom and watched for a while as the two witches indulged in each other for the sake of nothing more than pleasure. Not making magic. Not sating physical hunger. I might be a sentimental, old romantic, but it was beautiful.

When I joined them in the conversation about condoms, standing in the pool, Water Boy looked pleased to see me, whereas Earth was surprised and grabbed a towel to cover her naked body. She needn't have bothered.

"There are no condoms down here because, as a vampire, I do not need them. I'm unable to contract or transmit any human diseases or father a child. And, before today, I've never had two mortals together in here. By the way, I'm pleased to see you are enjoying my well-equipped facilities."

Her skin had turned pink with heat and embarrassment. The blood near the surface was a particularly attractive look on her. She smelt good, too.

"Are you're saying if you fuck me, I can't get pregnant or a disease? Do vampires fuck?" Malka's gaze dropped to my crotch.

What did she think I kept in there? "Yes. We fuck. And, yes, there'd be no risk to you if you had sex with a vampire without a condom," I confirmed. "At least, not from the sex itself. Depending on the vampire, there's a strong chance they'd bite down and kill you. A vampire might get lost in the moment, drain you of blood and kill you, or leave you with a fatal wound. So the moral of the tale is to pick your vampire lovers carefully. Make sure they have good self-control."

For much of the time I'd been in her company, the provocative odor of her desire enticed me. Now the much stronger aroma of sex surrounded us: hers and his. The scent danced around my nose and teased my tongue. I enjoyed fucking women and men, both equally and second only to how much I loved their blood. Blood and sex with these two witches would be the equivalent of vampire heaven. I'd maintain self-control for an indulgent drink of that.

"Oh, I almost forgot, you're gay." She let the towel drop that she'd been holding up over her.

"No, I'm not gay. I think the modern term is pansexual. Gender isn't an issue for me. Species is of interest, and what type of blood runs through my lovers' veins."

"So do you want to? Fuck me, I mean. Since Beck won't, it's against his religion."

The man in the water slapped her thigh playfully. "Not a religion."

She blew him a kiss. "After all, I've already told you I'd like a threesome with you two guys. I was serious." Malka was feisty and said what she thought regardless, and I liked her more for that.

It fascinated me that people confess things at the height of their sexual arousal that they might not otherwise admit to.

"Yes. But first, Malka, you must assure us you aren't a virgin." The scent of her blood already gave me the answer. I asked for Beck's sake, not my own. If they hadn't discussed it in my absence, the uncertainty would bother him.

Amused by the question, she laughed and choked and shook her head all at the same time. "You can't be serious. I'm almost twenty-one. How many virgins do you know in their twenties who invite guys for a threesome?"

I winked at Beck, and he smiled back at me. "They're pretty rare, I'll admit."

There was definitely a stirring down below, but I didn't work the same way as mortal men.

Still waist-deep in the water with his hands resting on her thighs, Beck knew what I needed. "You haven't eaten, have you?" he asked.

I didn't need to see his erection to know how turned on he was after making Malka come; I saw it in the warm flush of his skin, in the redness of his lips, in the blackness of his eyes. I'd seen him that way before when just the two of us were alone on many previous occasions.

The things Beck and I would have done if we'd have been alone didn't bear thinking about. There are many erotic ways of passing the time that don't include penetration. Now, for the first time, we had a third person with us. And she wanted both of us.

Vampire arousal isn't measured in erect inches; our bodies work differently. And ultimately, desire is in the mind. "I'd love to fuck you, Malka, but I'm running on empty. Light on blood, you know." I placed my hand on my flaccid cock through my clothes. "One of the downsides of being a vampire is that I can't get an erection if I haven't any blood to fill it." My eyes flickered at Beck.

She looked a little alarmed, which I guess is only to be understood as she knew so little about us.

"You've already heard me promise Fire I won't bite you, so there's only one of you I can drink from."

He groaned as if it were already happening.

Still staring at me, she gasped, wide-eyed with shock. "Will you drink Beck's blood? Wouldn't it kill him?"

She had no idea how much he wanted it.

"It won't hurt him at all." I winked at Beck. "I'm told a vampire bite can be orgasmic."

Beck patted her knee reassuringly. "It's okay. He's done it before. It's very, um, pleasant."

"I think he means erotic," I explained.

"Yes, that. I want it to happen, Malka. You also said earlier you wanted to see us fuck. Well, we won't do that, not exactly, but it's the next best thing."

"Flaming Haydn isn't the boss of me and my blood and who drinks it. If it's so orgasmic, you are welcome to drink my blood," Malka said.

Vampire heaven might be when two gorgeous young elementals both offered their blood for drinking and their bodies for sex at the same time.

"Hold on, the two of you, or I'll think it's my birthday. Which it can't be because I'm a Taurus. I'm not going to break my promise to Fire. I don't want him as my enemy, so the promise will stand for tonight. And I don't want you to get the wrong idea. It's not always erotic. There are many vampires who'd kill you. They wouldn't stop drinking until you were dead."

There were a bunch of vampires at the end of the road baying for blood, and there was nothing sexy about them.

The water witch placed his palms flat on the edge of the pool and slowly raised himself out of the water. His entire wet body glistened as droplets of water streamed down his smooth skin. Standing out perpendicular to his body, his long, hard cock looked as big and lovely as I'd ever seen it.

"Admit it, vampire, it's good between us because you love me."

We both knew he was joking. *Many a true word is spoken in jest.*

I doubted if he knew my feelings for him ran deeper than I could explain. I choose not to think about how much this young water elemental meant to me. Since I found him, he shook my world.

Heaven help me; he tempted me so.

Malka obviously thought so too. Open-mouthed, she'd watch him in just the same way as I.

When he stood on the edge of the pool with his hard cock just above her face, she responded faster than me, which is saying something. Licking her lips, she raised herself up on to her knees and licked across the crown. Her tongue extended further, and she twirled it around the glans.

He watched her for a moment before his eyes rolled back; he closed them, and another groan escaped him.

She sealed her lips against the end of his dick, kissing the head and then opening up to suck him in. It looked beautiful. I wanted to join her there, tasting her tongue and his cock in my mouth.

If I was going to join this party, I'd have to take what he offered first. I moved to stand beside him and ran my fingers down his cheek, gently turning his face toward mine before cupping his chin with one hand and holding the back of his head with the other. I brushed my lips over his, a familiar action that I craved all too often.

With our lips locked in a kiss and our tongues exploring each other's mouths, I ran a hand down his neck, over his clavicle, and across his chest. It rose and fell quickly with the pace of his breathing. He had a magnificent body to behold and to caress. Hungry as I was, I still liked to play with my food.

I kept my mouth on his skin, licking over his cheek and then nibbling his earlobe after breaking away from the kiss. At the same time, I stepped around him. I wanted to hold him against me, to feel his body against mine, and to take his weight in my arms; standing before him wasn't an option while Malka was on her knees, and I would not interrupt that.

When I was behind, I wrapped my arms around him; one arm across his chest, the other hand lower, and as close to his groin as possible without separating him from the girl.

Her scent told me how much she enjoyed all of this.

Resting my face against his neck, I licked and sniffed him for the longest time. It wasn't inevitable that he'd come shortly after my bite, but it was extremely likely. My bites alone wouldn't bring on orgasms, but with everything else that was going on and had already happened, I suspected it might bring about the tipping point this time.

It made no difference.

He'd tasted delicious to me before, during, or after his orgasm. I delayed it only for his enjoyment.

My teeth scratched over the surface of his skin, and I reached down to hold his cock at the base. The right squeeze just might delay his orgasm if it wasn't already too late. I came into contact with her hands, already holding his balls. Her lips brushed my fist.

Sensing the pulsing blood under the surface, I licked over the scratch and braced my arm around his chest, ready to catch him if he stumbled when I penetrated his skin.

My fangs pierced him easily, like a hot knife dipping into melted butter.

Warm, thick, pulsing blood filled my mouth.

Arousal.

Youthful enthusiasm.

Magic.

Great power over water.

Love.

I tasted it all when I drank from him. His guard dropped, and he showed me everything. He shared himself with me. His soul. His fears. His desires. His essence wrapped up in this intoxicating elixir.

The blood of a fifth-order elemental would always be a treat to respect, savor, and enjoy as long as Beck was willing to feed me. A reminder of why I had to keep him safe and close to me. But it was even more special now, whilst he tasted virginal. That wouldn't last, not now she had arrived.

Mindful not to take any more blood than I needed, and not to spill a drop of the valuable commodity, I sealed the wound long before I wanted to. Having no impact on my donor, I took enough to sustain me and enable me to perform.

I'd been so focused on what he was giving me, for those seconds, that I'd lost track of my surroundings, which could have been a dangerous lapse in any other place. The magical wards set around this room made it safer than any high-tech panic room and as safe as the room where I slept.

Here it simply meant I hadn't noticed how Beck had sagged a little in my arms.

What I gave him was better than any mere physical experience he had with witches, I was sure of that. I might have been just a tad envious about what he shared with the witches in his life, Fire and now Earth, but I wasn't a witch and couldn't replace them just as they could never replace me.

Still, I was fully aware that Fire, in turn, was most displeased by the continued relationship between Beck and me. I don't know which part Fire disapproved of most: that Water Boy freely offered me elemental blood, the physical aspect, or our friendship. All in all, it contributed to Fire's animosity toward me.

I derived great delight from how much Fire would disapprove of what was going on.

He wasn't excluded. He was just too up his own arse to join in.

Wickedly, I took a perverse delight in the fact that Beck and I shared intimacy with the woman that Fire had been waiting for.

This was the first time in years that anyone had come into this space apart from Beck and me. This oasis in my house was a place I shared with him and him alone.

Though unaware of it, Beck had imbued the wet area with his essence. Strong magic emanated from him and filled the room.

Vampires could sense magic, and sometimes use it, but we didn't create it.

You didn't get to be an old vampire and mix with many witches over the centuries without knowing how to harness their powers for your own benefit. How else would I have survived for so long while others fell at the hands of vampire hunters?

I'd not been attentive to all that was going on. I'd closed my eyes and snapped them open to see Malka had moved away.

Sitting up on a nearby rock that had been carved as a seat, her hand held her woman's parts. She watched, captivated. Unlike most witches, she wasn't disgusted by by my vampirism, which she'd just witnessed. All my senses told me she was still turned on. And the man in my arms hadn't come yet, either.

With my face still pressed against his neck, my rock-hard cock strained in my pants against his backside.

My grip tightened around his shaft, and slowly I dragged his foreskin back and forth. His precum dribbled onto my fingers.

We could go on. It wouldn't be the first time Beck and I had played in this room, but we'd never played with a third person.

"Thank you for that." Trying to sound casual, as if he'd lent me ten pounds. I kissed his neck, it being the only way I could tell him it meant more. The thought of losing him terrified me. If the local vampires had their way, they'd rip the witches from Summer House Road.

If I could tell the Water Boy everything, I'd tell him I loved him, and I'd keep him safe. I'd tell him I couldn't bear to lose him in the way that my last great love was taken. His existence upon this world was ripped from him by a mere boy child with a knife.

Instead, I whispered loud enough for her to hear, "Now we have a lady to satisfy."

He stood up straight, supporting his own weight, and rolled his shoulders back. "I'm ready for that."

CHAPTER FOURTEEN

So Hot with a capital H
Malka Selby

I FIGURED IF BECK DIDN'T want me sucking his cock, he'd push me away and give me a better explanation about what was on and off-limits when you're 'saving yourself' for sex magic.

When I sat back, the vampire bite looked like a kiss. One intense, lingering, sexy kiss. A kiss between two men in love. I wanted to understand what turned Beck to putty and made him craving more.

No matter what they said about meeting in a gay bar and then letting me believe that nothing much happened, there must have been far more to their story than they'd told me.

Chemistry like that didn't spring spontaneously from nowhere.

Fully dressed, the dark, dominant Romanian held the naked, muscular man as if he'd never let him get away. The blond Brit's dick filled the Romanian's hand.

Opposites attract.

The scene was a hot and erotic tableau.

From now on, I wanted my threesomes always to involve guys who enjoyed snogging and holding each other like that. Kissing each other *all* over wouldn't go amiss.

They'd already suggested that Varu's bite was orgasmic, and it was no joke; I saw the effect it had on Beck. His whole body visibly tensed and relaxed as if he were going to come. He must have been close. His diamond-hard dick twitched and jerked. His eyes screwed shut, his mouth gaped open, and a blissed-out expression took residence on his face.

It looked Hot with a capital H.

It wasn't just Beck. Varu held him so close it appeared the vampire wanted the water witch in all ways, and not only for his blood.

I felt privileged to view this intimate moment, and not at all self-conscious touching my wet place while I watched them.

Varu's lip's left the skin's surface, and his tongue swiped over the place where he must have bitten. He'd finished, licked his red lips, and stepped back from Beck as if the man meant nothing to him. But that was not how it really looked to me.

"Did you drink his blood right then? Because I don't see any blood, and it looked like you were giving him a love bite."

The spell between them was broken, and ignoring each other, they both looked at me. With my hand stroking over my girl parts, I felt like a deer caught in the headlights, but I had no wish to run away.

"Do you see a puncture wound?" asked the vampire.

"No. Nothing."

Unbuttoning his black shirt, Varu stepped toward me. "I'm ready to taste another witch in another way tonight." Grinning at me, the arrogant sexy vampire appeared young and, and held us both captivated. He had us eating from the palm of his old hand.

"Where and how shall we do this thing?" I asked, glancing around, looking for some place to get comfortable.

"I think we'd do best in the bedroom," Varu replied.

Beck stepped toward me, his manhood rigidly pointing in my direction, and it was impossible not to stare at it. "Come on, Malka, the guestroom is behind you."

Guestroom? Thank goodness Varu didn't mean the cave of dirt I'd seen earlier.

Beyond the indoor garden bathing pool cave, they took me to a spacious bedroom with an enormous wooden four-poster bed in the middle.

Even though we were underground with no windows, I hoped Varu intended for me to sleep here. The walls were painted white in the large room, and many tiny recessed lights shone like stars from the high ceiling.

"Is this where you bring back your stream of lovers? No, you don't have to answer." I didn't know why I said it. I didn't want to picture either of them with a string of lovers. It was just... sometimes, words fell from my mouth before they were thought through.

"Beck's been here before," Varu said cryptically. There had to be something more to their relationship. I'd seen how they interacted. They looked like lovers.

Varu was a vampire: I was increasingly inclined to accept his story.

Beck was a witch; I'd seen him do magic that I couldn't explain, and he saved himself for sex-magic, whatever that meant. I didn't have much idea.

I wasn't sure if the two could mix and date when they were supposedly at war. I supposed it might be a Romeo and Juliet story, though it was tough to imagine Beck as a virginal teenage Juliet.

I sat down on the edge of the bed and faced the two men who were both now naked and giving slow strokes to their hard dicks. I wouldn't have minded watching them do that to each other, but there might be a limit to how much I'd want to watch without joining in.

"If you don't mind, as it is my bedroom and I'm the eldest, I suggest I also direct the fun."

If I were directing, I'd have asked them to touch each other's cock, but I didn't mind waiting to find out how it would play out with Varu in charge. "Okay. How do you want to fuck me?" I asked.

"On your knees. I will take you from behind while you suck Beck's cock."

"Yes, sir." I instantly turned on to my knees with my legs apart and wiggled my ass, giving him a full view of my invitation before he changed his mind.

"Are you both going to come in me?"

"Do you want us to?" Varu asked.

Hell, yes. It sounded filthy. I'd done nothing like this before. If I was to be the mid-piece in a spit-roast, I wanted it all. "What do you want?" I looked at Beck. "Coming in my mouth or pulling out to come over my face?"

"You're killing me, Malka. Stop talking dirty or I'll come too soon." He sat down on the bed in front of me and spread his long legs apart so they were on either side of me.

I glanced over my shoulder. "What about for you, Varu? In me or on me? Which is sexiest?"

"If I wasn't undead, you'd be killing me, too. Now, if you truly don't mind, we'll surprise you."

"I don't mind, just fuck me already."

Beck got on the bed in front of me, and for the second time, I teased his dick with my tongue. My jaws were going to ache the next day after filling my mouth with this big boy.

This time, however, it was harder to concentrate because Varu's erection was equally impressive. And I felt every inch as he stretched and entered me. I didn't recall ever being with such well-hung men.

Varu entered slowly with care, but I wanted hard and fast. I pushed back on to him and appreciated that he'd offered me a position that gave me the scope to set the pace. I thrust back on Varu and forward on Beck. I wished for a mirror on the wall; I would have loved to watch us. But I was there, in person, and imagined what we looked like.

My clit throbbed, and if possible, my pussy got wetter. That might have been Beck's magic.

Varu's fingers rubbed over my clit, and that additional attention pushed me over when I reached the edge of another orgasm, which didn't take long.

When I needed to cry out so loud that anyone in the street might hear me, Beck's cock fell from my mouth. I simply couldn't give him attention and suck his cock right then through my orgasm. I wasn't sure how well soundproofed the underground room was, but I gave it my all, screaming my pleasure like a porn star.

And I collapsed on the bed, burying my head in the sheets that were also being twisted by my hands.

This must have been too much for my new lovers because splashes of warm cum landed across my back. A lot of it, and I wasn't sure who it produced it.

For a few seconds or minutes, I remained with my face buried in the clean-smelling cotton. At least these sheets smelled freshly laundered after whoever else he'd fucked in the bed.

And I attempted to recover. If I waited too long, I'd be embarrassed about my behavior. God. I'd never behaved like a slutty porn star before. It was fun and sexy, but now, after the fact, well, it might get embarrassing.

A head came down next to mine. Hot breath blew past my ear, and then Beck's voice. "That was so hot. Thank you."

"You liked it?" I whispered. Because suddenly, self-doubt rose within me, replacing my libido. I'd been over the top, and those guys might've had a better time without me. I saw how they were together.

"Yes. I liked it a lot," he answered.

"I've never done anything quite like it," I confessed. Now we'd finished, I wanted them both to know. "Never before."

"Then I need to ask you, Malka, did you enjoy it? I hope you did."

Without moving from where I lay, I nodded. "Thanks, guys," I said. Thanking people seemed to be the order of the day. A bit impersonal, but I'd roll with it.

I became vaguely aware of a warm damp cloth wiping the man-juice from my back. They were gentlemen; of course, they weren't just going to leave me to clean myself up.

"I should go home."

All right, Beck didn't want to stay the night.

"I need to see Haydn," he said.

Why?

"I also have to leave for a while, Malka, but you will be safe sleeping here. I'd be back soon. There are things I'd like to show you before sunrise, so you should rest now."

And Varu intended to leave too.

"Why?" I didn't intend to say it aloud.

So, perhaps they were both going to leave me once they'd had their fun.

Oh, wait. I had fun. I initiated it. And I was done with them. The previous threesome guys had spent the night cuddling and sleeping with me. I liked it, but I didn't need that.

"I imagine you'd like some fresh clothes, and I have nothing to fit you," Varu said. He had a point. The clothes I'd been wearing had been rolled in cemetery earth, and my spare clothes stored back in King's Cross were all in need of laundering too.

Exhaustion took me to sleep without allowing time for goodbyes. I didn't hear the men leave the room.

I woke up a couple of hours later to find myself alone. A small lamp gave some illumination to the room, and on the bedside table I found a small pile of new clothes in my size. They were similar to what I'd been wearing, and with the labels still inside. Thoughtfully, Varu had left a pair of scissors atop along with a new toothbrush, still in the packet. When I got out of bed, I found a choice of two pairs of boots on the floor.

New clothes, a set for now and spare for later, were useful gifts, and made up for them not staying in bed with me.

Once I stirred, after all that had happened since I stepped off the bus in Dalston less than twelve hours earlier, it was impossible to return to sleep. My brain worked overtime thinking things through.

It turned out Uncle Byrne was not my uncle—he was my legal guardian, an asshole, and a witch.

I still had to find out the details of the trust fund that I stood to benefit from after my twenty-first birthday. My future waited for me to pick it up. Still, it seemed it was about to take a dramatically different course to what I ever envisioned, not least because my family wealth seemed far greater than I imagined. The property portfolio wasn't the only legacy.

Either all the people around Summer House Road were barking mad, or I'd fucked a vampire.

The next conversation I had with Betty, my around-the-world travel-pal, was impossible to imagine. What would we say after we'd compare notes on menages, and I told her I was a witch?

She'd tell me about how her family was doing while, at the same time, deciding I'd lost grip with reality. I'd tell her about vampires and magic, and she'd call the men with white coats to bring a straight jacket. I'd be locked away like my mom before I killed anyone.

Returning to King's Cross, where I'd left my stuff, and checking back into the same hotel seemed an excellent plan. The thought that I might run into those guys on the third floor did *NOT* cross my mind. Not too much.

To find out about my trust fund, I'd visit so-called Uncle Byrne in daylight when I had a little more time to process all this. Reflecting on life from a neutral distance was preferable to spending the entire night in a vampire's basement, no matter how luxurious.

I found myself closing the door quietly behind me in the dark early hours of the morning and walking toward the end of Summer House Road. A bunch of people milled about at the far end of the road. Optimistically, I hoped to find a black cab or a minicab office or a night bus along the main road, which would take me the five or so miles from Stoke Newington to King's Cross.

CHAPTER FIFTEEN

The irresistible temptation of blood freshly squeezed from a virgin
Varu Vasile

SHORTLY BEFORE THE shops closed, I made it to Westfield shopping emporium.

The staff were attempting to usher dawdling browsers out of my chosen store and stared coldly at the people outside to deter any intending to enter when there were only minutes until closing.

Paying no heed, I zoomed past, moving faster than their eyes could track and coming to a halt within the heart of women's clothing.

Glancing at my watch, I approached the nearest female sales assistant, a middle-aged woman—Lucy, according to her name badge. "I only have a minute, and I need a complete new outfit for my friend. In fact, two sets. Including underwear, socks, and boots." Which was why this task needed a female perspective.

At the same time as whipping out my phone to show her the pictures I'd taken, I pulled out my wallet to demonstrate the serious nature of this shopping expedition. "I'd like two more sets of clothes, just like these. The closest match." The photographs showed the labels, so the sales lady had product codes, brands, and sizes.

"We have an enormous range of jeans to choose from." Lucy frowned. "Color, cut, detailing."

"You choose just the closest things to those that I'm showing you. Exactly the same will be fine if you have it, Lucy. And she needs underwear too." I hadn't taken a photograph of her smalls.

"Undergarments that are practical for everyday situations. Whatever you'd wear if you were a kick-ass vampire slayer and zombie hunter."

The assistant giggled. "I know the very knickers you're looking for. I'll be right back."

"Should I be worried?" I said to her back as I followed her toward ladies' lingerie.

"Only if you are a zombie or a vampire." She clearly had a sense of humor. The woman knew her job. She picked up items on hangers at an impressive speed, for a human, gathering jeans and tops before we reached panties and socks.

While Lucy gathered clothing, a beautiful red dress caught my eye. It wasn't practical for fighting vampires and demons or for everyday wear, but the shade would look lovely against her skin. I picked up what I guessed to be the correct size and asked Lucy to find shoes, underwear, and a jacket to go with it.

Finally, the entire wardrobe came together. Laden down with bags, I deposited them at home before checking on the Turkish vampires and possibly securing another drop of human blood before sunrise.

After dropping the items in Malka's room whilst she slept soundly, I went out again. I passed through the cemetery, but this time I doubled back along Stoke Newington Church Street to approach Summer House Road from the other side of the divide.

Most of the crowd that had been there earlier had dispersed. There were just a few vampires lingering near the end of my road, presumably stationed there to pick up Malka if she tried to leave. They ignored me as if they hadn't sensed me. Maybe they hadn't. I had nothing about me to draw their attention.

Three vampires loitered on the street, ready to take Malka off my hands if I brought her to them, but there was plenty of time for that. They wouldn't expect me to hand her over anytime soon when they'd allowed me forty-eight hours with the young witch.

No vampire would part from elemental blood sooner than they had to.

Of greater interest to me right then: the scent of the virgins still lingered in the air. They were near, or had only departed very recently. Their odor captivated me, and it would distract all the vampires in the area.

If I were among this Turkish group and wanted to persuade a resident vampire to capture and surrender a local naïve witch, I'd keep the prized virgin blood within close range as a constant reminder of the prize.

It was temptation indeed, and one I was unlikely to resist.

Any vampires forced to endure the scent continuously would struggle to maintain rational judgment unless they had a ready supply of superior quality blood to feed upon.

I did.

Beck wasn't only a virgin, but an elemental and a powerful witch of the fifth order. More powerful elementals were few and far between. Not that I ever told him this. It wouldn't do to volunteer too much information to other people regardless of my relationship with them. Beck had to discover his power in his own good time as he learned how to use and control it.

Richer blood than his would be a rare find indeed. Nevertheless, I wouldn't say no to drinking from these humans as well. I could practically taste them via their scent, and that wasn't enough.

Curiosity had me wondering about the humans' accessibility and how the Turkish vampires resisted taking the prize for themselves.

My senses gave me the answers as I neared. Either the Supreme High Priestess had lured the Turks to do her dirty work by offering blood of such quality to them, or they were taking it, anyway.

The human virgins had left the street recently and not gone far. I turned my attention to the surrounding buildings. The delicious scent oozed out of a house opposite.

A ground floor sash window stood open, inviting attention from opportunist burglars. They had intentionally left the window open to lure me in. They wanted me to know about the delicacies within. I had no doubt the humans were just on the other side of the curtain.

Ignoring the vampires on the street, I made my way toward the scent of virgin blood exposed to air and drying on naked, human skin.

My head passed through the opening in an instant. The room was in darkness. Like all the vampires already present, I had unhindered vision in the room. Not that I needed my eyes to confirm what my other senses had told me.

Anyone of the vampires could have drained all three people, but the six vampires in the room held back. None of them wanted to pay the penalty for killing valuable assets. From their restraint, I'd wager they didn't have permission to drink much, if any, of the virgin blood.

However, their vampire senses and natural urges triumphed over any rules to abstain fully. They had the three humans tethered to chairs, paper-sharp gashes cut into their exposed thighs and upper arms. Blood bubbled to the surface of the thighs, mostly dried, contributing to the perfume in the air.

Gravity drew droplets of blood down from the vertical slices in the arms. Vampires sat close by, enthralled. My entering the room through the window didn't distract them from their focus on the blood. They acted as if I wasn't there, but they were aware of me.

They drew mere drops of red liquid from the flesh, and the vampires watched as hungrily as humans captivated by TV cooking shows. The vampires kept their eyes on the humans. Out of their minds with longing, the six vampires took turns to lap at the trickling blood that dribbled down the arms. Not a drop spilled from the elbows to the floor.

As a whole, the display was wasteful and decadent. It wasn't about nourishment but about savoring everything sensual about the very best blood. Given permission, I'd no doubt the vampires would have reverted to instinct, ripped the humans to shreds, and basked in the vital fluid.

I was no different from my fellow vampires.

I assessed how I might get a part of this action and whether I had any chance of taking a person entirely for myself.

The sound of a door opening and closing followed by footsteps in the street outside didn't warrant my attention. They were common enough sounds. The scent and the aura, however, were distinctive.

For a second or two, I assumed her scent was in my nose because I wore it. It lingered on my skin and clothes. The force of her aura, however, bore down on us like a change in air pressure. It was unmissable. All the vampires in the area would know the young witch was outside again.

As fast as I could move, which was faster than anything I could think of, I was out of the window.

If I stayed here at the end of the road, I'd watch Malka proceed toward me to meet her fate as she walked into the waiting arms of the vampires.

I couldn't cross that line of salt to prevent her from coming closer.

From this side of the line, I could only help the Turks, and the Supreme High Priestess, by implication.

I had no choice but to race at full speed along Church Street. I went through the cemetery at top speed, sinking through the earth adjacent to my home, and resurfacing in my back garden. I opened my back door and ran through the house. Leaving my front door gaping open, I dashed onto Summer House Road, at the same time, calling out her name at the top of my voice and hoping it was enough.

"Malka!"

I wasn't too late.

She still stood there at the end of the road, and she'd be over the line if she took just one more step. The vampires hid out of sight so as not to deter her, but they'd be waiting to pounce the instant she crossed the magical line of safety.

"Malka, wait!"

She stopped, but before she could turn, one of the young female vampires came into view. "Excuse me, miss," she politely addressed the witch. "I'm a little lost. Do you know which direction Islington is from here?" She held her phone, presumably with a map on the screen—an appeal to the helpful nature of the prey.

CHAPTER SIXTEEN

The great escape from the vampire's lair
Malka Selby

VARU RAN OUT OF HIS front door, calling my name. I'd just left from there, and I had no idea he was in the house. Half a second later, he was by my side and giving a lady directions to Islington.

I wanted to help, but I'd be no good looking at directions or a map on the screen of a mobile phone. I used paper maps, much to the amazement of most people my age.

Half a second? I didn't time it; that was just an estimation based on him being a mind-bogglingly fast runner, like, a speed of light blur. As if he didn't move but materialized instantly in the place he wanted to be. And yet, the lost woman didn't seem surprised that a man appeared out of nowhere. She must've been drunk or on drugs.

"Shall we walk with her? Make sure she's okay?" I asked Varu. I wasn't sure how safe this street was for a woman on her own even though I'd just set off by myself. At least I was compos mentis.

"No. She'll be fine." He put a firm hand on my shoulder and turned me to face him. "I don't mind if you want to leave. You're free to go. But before you do, I have something back at the house that I want to show you."

Despite the words, I had a strong sense he didn't want me going anywhere. I barely knew Varu, but I had the impression there was a whole hidden subtext behind everything he said and did.

I couldn't quite put my finger on it, but the impression that he had things to hide made me uneasy.

Of course, I understood why he didn't reveal his true vampire identity when we first met, but why would he want to keep me in at his place now? In addition, I suspected there was more to the love tangle between him and Beck and Haydn than he'd told me.

We set off back to his home.

My stomach rumbled. I hadn't eaten anything in a long while. "I was coming back. I just wanted go get some food," I lied, feeling guilty at leaving without saying goodbye after the way he'd bought new clothes for me and chased after me. "I thought I'd find a late-night takeaway place around here."

"Maria has prepared food for you."

"She has?" I had no idea when that happened. I blushed at the thought of Maria cooking while we had group sex in the sub-basement.

We were halfway back to the house when the heavens opened and drenched us in a sudden torrential downpour. I ran the rest of the way, just a hundred yards or so, but far enough for my footfalls to splash in the rapidly forming puddles. Varu kept pace next to me rather than running ahead.

When I neared the end of the street, Maria held open the front door. I walked in and removed my dirty new boots, leaving them next to the front door. I didn't want to walk wet, muddy footprints through the house. I wasn't raised that way.

Without removing his footwear, Varu took me into the front room where we'd sat earlier. Someone had tidied the room. Beck's chair had been returned to the table, the drinking glasses were gone, replaced by a place set with cutlery at the table for one person to dine. Varu invited me to sit there. He sat opposite. From that position, I looked at the old wooden display cabinets that were over-filled with little ornaments. It all looked dated, worn, and kitsch, as distinct from ancient and antique.

Maria entered carrying a glass, a jug of water, and a small plate of food on a tray. She set the glass and pitcher on the table and placed the food before me. The unfamiliar little sausage-shaped offerings looked delicious.

"Sarmale to start." She answered my unspoken question. "For the main, I can offer beef stew, or I'd be happy to prepare something else if you'd prefer?"

It seemed odd to eat stew in the middle of the night, but I was hungry, and my body clock was out of sync, so I said, "Stew would be lovely, thank you."

My need for food was more urgent than my need to deal with the unpleasant feeling of being a little cold and damp. Varu didn't seem to notice our damp clothes.

When Maria left the room, I looked at him. "You aren't eating, of course. What are these? Do you know?" I picked up the morsel of food with my fork and took a bite without waiting for an answer.

"My servants are Romanian, and this is typical of their food. It is called sarmale. She cooks big batches of them. Same with the stew."

I got the name, I was still none the wiser about what they actually were. But they were tasty and warm. "Is that deliberate? Servants from your home country?"

"Yes, I chose them back in Romania, and they came with me." I thought he'd been here for centuries, but he may have gone back to visit from time to time.

I tucked in hungrily. The sarmale was a little spicier than I anticipated, but really not bad at all. "It seems strange, you not eating. I had etiquette drilled into me at school, but we learned nothing about sitting down to eat when a vampire is in the room. Like whether you'd know about food. Do I talk to you about it? Do we pretend I'm not eating, or do I tell you how good it is and that you don't know what you're missing?"

He waved his hand dismissively. "Think nothing of it. You and I eat different things."

He was right. That didn't take any thinking about.

"And you need to keep your strength up. It's going to be a busy couple of days."

"What makes you say that? I planned on going back to my hotel room and sleeping for forty-eight hours after I meet with Haydn and find out what's going on."

Varu smiled knowingly. "You hope you'll understand what's going on after meeting Haydn. Let me know how that goes."

"What aren't you telling me, Varu?"

He raised his shoulders. "Eat up," he said as Maria entered carrying another tray. This time she brought a huge bowl of stew, enough for two people. There were additional side plates of bread and potatoes. Again, the warm herbs and spices smelled heavenly. I was so so hungry.

I surveyed the food, wondering about the best way to tackle it. "Don't just sit and watch me eat, tell me about you and Beck and Haydn." And I dug into the stew with the spoon.

"Tell you what?"

"Why aren't you and Beck a couple?"

Varu snorted with laughter. "We're a totally different species. Somewhat similar, granted, but he'll be old and die in no time compared to how long I will live."

I swallowed the hot stew. "But you look good together. You make each other happy. You care about him. And then, you and Haydn are so, um... what's the word, *antagonistic*... toward each other? Yet you pushed Beck to live with Haydn. That's what I don't understand. You like one man, don't like the other, and you push the two together when one's a complete and utter jerk."

Varu laughed. "Haydn's an ass, but he's what Beck wants and needs."

"Bullshit. He wants you," I blurted out.

Varu's mouth curved upward, but the smile didn't reach his eyes. He shook his head but took a while before answering. "You are jumping to conclusions based on what you've seen. You've seen Beck with me. Yes, I care for him and he for me, but we will never be like a romantic couple from fiction. If you consider what you saw, I also saw Beck with you, and he seems to like you a lot too."

"Huh," I grunted. *That was just a bit of fun.*

"And, wait until you see Beck with Haydn."

Chewing on my food, I considered Varu's words. "Are you saying Beck has the hots for Haydn too? Oh my god, you need to step between them. Beck shouldn't fall in love with that violent jerk."

"I'd say they love each other already. If they were ordinary humans, they might even be planning their wedding, but Haydn's bound to you. They've both been anxious about your arrival here and how that will change everything."

I sputtered; in fact, I choked on my food. "In what way might I change things?" I spat out after sipping water. *And how can I be in the way of them getting married?*

"We'll have to see. Just like Beck once did, you now need Haydn to help you survive as an elemental."

And that mysterious way of talking was so annoying about Varu. I sensed he knew more than he ever said, and he dropped hints but didn't follow through. "Just tell me, why does Beck look like he's in love with you? And why did he take part in a threesome with the two of us if he's in love with Haydn? That's something I don't understand." And didn't accept. There was no way I'd accept Beck and Haydn were a couple.

"As I said, those two witches have never made a single-minded commitment to each other because of you. Miss Selby, the relationships that Water has with myself and with Fire isn't like those you have learned about in romantic fiction. We are nothing like Jane Austen's characters, or Cinderella and her prince. We aren't seeking one true love. Fire and I are both friends with Beck. We both care about him. At my age, I've had many lovers and seen them die, yet my existence goes on and on. With great age comes the great ability to share."

"You aren't jealous about Beck and Haydn?"

"A tad, sometimes." He shook his head, a smile on his face, as always, as if I'd said something amusing. "Loving relationships don't have to be exclusively between two people. More people involved doesn't dilute a relationship. It can make it stronger. Affection is not like a pan of meat stew that gets emptier as you eat; it is more like blood, it is unlimited."

"Think I'll stick with stew, thanks."

"For Beck, he has two deep friendships with two men who care for him. As for Fire, well, I don't much like the fire witch, and that's mutual. But in his way, he greatly cares for Beck. For me, I care about Beck, so I'm pleased he has more than just me in his life. I can't provide everything he needs. I can't always be there for him. I can't offer him everything, and I can't always protect him. And, likewise, I don't expect him to be everything for me."

"You sound so wise." I didn't expect him to say so much. "Oh. And how do I fit in? You said I'd change things."

"You will. Haydn won't commit to Beck because he's waiting for you to turn up and take your place at the head of the Summer House Coven. You might bless their relationship, encourage it, or bring it to an end through the choices you make."

"What if I don't want to head the coven?" I'd only just discovered I was a witch, and I wasn't sure about that at all. Surely I wasn't expected to take up some witchcraft responsibilities as well.

"What you do is up to you, but there are some things that you can't avoid. You were born an elemental, you will become a powerful witch, and you are heir to the Selby estate. Of course, your mother might return and take her place as High Priestess, or you can produce an heir. It will be easier to explain by showing you when you are ready to leave the table."

"I'm ready." I'd made a big dent in the pile of food placed before me though I couldn't possibly eat it all.

Varu pushed back from the table. "We must descend."

CHAPTER SEVENTEEN

The earthy sleeping chamber or dirty panic room
Malka Selby

WEARING ONLY NAVY BLUE cotton socks on my feet, I followed Varu down the stairs, descending below his house once again.

He stopped at a place where I'd felt guilty earlier and guilty now. I wondered if Maria and the man had told Varu they'd seen us snooping. He might be about to challenge me for prying in his bedroom. I wondered if I should own up before he said anything.

Hey, I didn't know that was your bedroom. Beck showed it to me. In my head, it sounded stupid.

Varu watched my face as he opened the door. "What do you see?"

"Just black dirt," I answered slowly.

He switched his weight from one foot to another as though deep in thought. "Um, describe in more detail exactly what's there."

"An empty room. It's dark. The walls, floor, and ceiling are all loose dirt, from what I can tell. It looks like a freshly plowed field, not flattened like a track."

"And how deep is the room?"

"I don't know. It's hard to tell. Two or three beds might fit in lengthwise. I guess that would make it twenty feet deep and perhaps ten or fifteen feet wide. It's hard to tell from out here."

Varu stepped in, holding out his hand, inviting me to join him.

Looking down at my new socks that hadn't been on my feet all that long, I decided to take them off and wash my feet later. I pushed off each sock with the opposite foot, much to Varu's amusement, took his hand, and stepped on to the soft soil.

We walked deeper into the dark space. A breeze whipped about the room, sending my hair over my face. I let go of Varu, swept my hair back into place, and crossed my arms in front of me.

"There are no windows down here," he said.

"Yes. Obviously." I sounded like a teenager as I looked at him blankly. His point was what?

"The wind is due to your mother's magic. Very few witches can do what you just did."

Startled, I looked around, wondering what he was talking about and what it had to do with my mother. "What did I just do?" I looked at my feet to see if I'd sunk into the ground again. "I've followed you on the stairs. Had a threesome with two passionate guys who are also supernatural creatures. What else?"

He laughed. "Stepping this far into my room, or even seeing inside it, is something most witches can't do, and I don't know why you can. I'm not sure if it is your magic or because you are your mother's daughter. When people open that door, they see a small space just a foot or two deep, nothing more than a broom cupboard lined with soil. That's what Maria sees, and that's what Beck told me he saw when I showed him where I sleep."

It hadn't crossed my mind that when I looked at something the person standing next to me would perceive something so very different. But that was what Varu implied about the conversation I'd had about this room with Beck earlier.

"Well, that explains why he won't just stick with you. You know how to push a man away by making him think you sleep in a dirty little cupboard."

Of course, Varu raised an eyebrow and smiled. "You'll notice, Water Boy knew the way to the guest room. I only sleep here. When

I opened the door to this room, he saw a shallow cupboard. I allowed him to believe that there was nothing more to my sleeping quarters."

It was mind-boggling to discover Beck and I had looked in earlier and had a conversation about this room, but it turned out we were discussing different things.

"No one apart from me has been in here since Serina."

"Ew." My face wrinkled in disgust. "Don't tell me you also slept with my mother?" I shuddered.

He shook his head. "No. We've never." For once, he didn't smirk, but appeared disturbed at the notion.

"Then how do I see something different from other people?"

"Of course, this space is real to us. We're standing in it. That's Romanian soil beneath your feet. We passed through the false illusion of the back of the closet. We've walked through a wall of earth. Not dissimilar to when you fell through the ground in the cemetery and passed right through to my cellar."

"So, you're telling me that there's a wall of earth somewhere over there, but I'm not aware of it, and I passed through it? How is that possible?" Squinting to see something that wasn't there, I stepped toward the door with my hands held out in front of me, trying to feel something. I found nothing. It sounded farfetched, but nothing, literally nothing, would surprise me anymore. Not after the day I'd had.

Without blinking or even smiling, Varu watched me. "You can't find it, can you?"

"So, you noticed." Smart arse.

"Even I see a solid wall of earth." He walked over and put his hand up, presumably touching this invisible wall. "I don't know why you can't see it as well. Both you and I are able to pass through the earth, but this is strange. We might need Serina to explain it, although I would hazard a few guesses."

"Do you want to share your best guess? The thing is, my mother is a bit busy right now; tied up, you could say."

"Perhaps you can see through the earth because you can pass through it like me, but I see it with vampire eyes. Different magic enables you to see and pass through. You're from a family of witches, and your mother put the enchantment on this room."

I wondered at the relationship between my mother and this vampire, who should have been arch enemies from what I'd learned, and yet they chose to live close to each other and help each other.

"I don't see through all earth. Falling through the ground in the cemetery felt gross, and I hope I won't do again in a hurry. I'm trying to forget it. It's not like it turned invisible."

"But the difference is I'm a vampire, and you're an earth witch. Our abilities are similar, but the source of our ability isn't the same. It might be to do with the wall being so thin or to do with the magical wards that protect this room. Wards set in place by your mother. The wall of earth should prevent humans, witches, and vampires from finding this space."

"Oh, this is your safe room? Like in the movie Panic Room with Jodie Foster?" My traveling companion, Betty, was a big Jodie Foster fan and had forced me to watch Jodie Foster's every film at some point. Betty said she was forcing me because her lesbian moms forced her to watch Jodie, and it never did her any harm.

He looked at me blankly.

"You may mock me about my lack of a mobile phone, but don't you watch movies?"

"I am a cinema man, actually. The snacks there are good for enjoying in the dark whilst watching the film, but I must have missed that one. Was it good?"

Best we don't talk about our food, after all. "Yes, pretty good. But why did my mad mother get involved in setting up a panic room for you? Who or what do you have to hide from? And how come I can just walk in as if I belong here?"

"I'm not sure why you can see in and walk in here. As for why? The answer's simple. Serina and I helped each other. I think I've already explained it makes sense to cooperate with your neighbors. I'm not sure if she intentionally granted access to blood of her blood. She may have foreseen that you might one day need access to a safe room. Or perhaps she never knew this would happen. It might be because you're an earth witch. I'm hoping it's not an overlooked weakness in my safety, because I don't want other witches as powerful as yourself stumbling in uninvited."

"That's a pretty big if. They'd have to be opening the doors to broom cupboards under the basement of a vampire's house in London." I couldn't believe I'd so quickly adapted to calling this man a vampire when I'd only met him a few hours earlier, and I had been very resistant to the label only a few hours ago. At that point, I thought 'vampire' was a term of insult because they only existed as bad guys in stories. "And it can't be anything to do with being powerful because I'm not magical at all. Anyway, is this room what you wanted to show me?"

"One of the things. I brought you here for another reason. Serina Selby's magic has protected the room for many years, and before she went to prison, your mother placed an item in here for safekeeping."

Looking around at the empty room, I felt skeptical. "What, a barrel of extra Romanian dirt?"

Varu cocked his head to one side and scraped his fingers through his short black hair. "Funny. No. A valuable magical item that belongs to your family. To you, actually. Are you aware of it?"

I looked again; my eyes strained to see anything other than black soil in the darkness. I imagined seeing spiders and other creepy crawlies, and my bare feet wanted to get out of there. I stepped toward the light coming through the open door, resisting the temptation to run.

"Malka, you need the item. It's yours."

I stopped. I thought I probably stood within the vicinity of the invisible wall of earth. I couldn't see a single grubby molecule of its existence. Nevertheless, I was pleased to be within a few steps of the exit. "I don't know where it is. Or what it is. What am I looking for?"

"You won't find it by looking with your eyes."

What else am I supposed to look with?

"I come into this room every day without seeing it, and I have excellent night vision. Your mother has hidden it. She was a powerful Air witch and I expect she still is. Now, her blood flows in your veins. Your magical potential is phenomenal; seventh order, no less. Your element is earth. This room is only earth and magic, nothing more. You can find it by using your senses."

Senses? I could try. I closed my eyes so I definitely wouldn't see spiders, and I wasn't going to think about them either. Senses? I listened. The pool was below us with the waterfall and pumped water, but I could hear nothing of it. "Does the magic stop sound entering and leaving the room? Can people outside hear you snoring if you sleep in here?"

"The room is soundproofed, to some extent. No sound leaves the room. But when we are inside, we can hear things beyond the room."

I closed my eyes again and listened. "I can't hear anything, just so you know."

I heard only my own heart beating and breath traveling through my nose. I didn't think any other sense would be useful. The scent of freshly turned earth filled my nose. The soft earth felt pleasant under my feet. From time to time, a breeze swirled around the room before dying down. He'd mentioned it being my mother's magic. I wondered if that happened to magic trapped inside a room and if it were trying to escape.

Nothing. That was what I could sense. "Nothing. I can't sense anything. I don't know how to tap into magic."

"You did it earlier and fell through the ground."

"But I don't know how I did it. At the time, I was running for my life in the dark through a graveyard."

"Don't think about it now either. Open your mind to unfamiliar feelings. The item is yours; it will call to you."

"What is it? It might help if I know what I'm looking for."

"It won't help, and I can't tell you."

My eyes closed again.

Truly, I wanted to believe in my ability to turn into a magical magnet and make items slowly move toward me. After a minute, I would open my eyes, and it would be there at my feet.

There was no surge of unfamiliar power. Nothing magical came at me from another dimension. I felt nothing. Nothing other than the sound of the warm wind flowing around the room. It drew tiny particles of earth from every surface and threw them into the currents of air. The odor of dirt became stronger. Its flavor, bitter and rich. Its gritty texture teased my tongue. Its metallic composition hit my nose and coated the back of my throat.

When I opened my eyes, the first thing I saw was my naked feet standing in the same coal-black dirt and, thankfully, no spiders.

"You are an earth elemental. A powerful witch. Anything concealed here in the earth, you can find it." Varu's pep talk carried the weight of his conviction, but I remained unconvinced. "Claim it, Malka, it's yours," he urged.

"I can't, okay? I've tried, and I can't find it. I don't know how to do magic." I doubted my ability. His insistence that I could do this thing was frustrating.

"You can do it. You can learn." Varu's voice was louder, with a forceful urgency to the tone. He wasn't quite shouting. "Some things you can do by instinct. Just as you passed through the earth, your amulet is here, Malka, and you need it. Take it."

"Look, I don't respond well to being bossed around," I snapped. Or being shouted at, for that matter. Not since I got out of that awful school. "And I don't know what an amulet is, or why I should want it, anyway. I want to go downstairs and wash my feet, and go to bed with a drink. Do you have any alcohol?"

Varu shook his head.

Standing at the far end of the room, his face was in shadow, and I sensed his pleasant mood had gone. His commands for me to use magic sounded stern. Whatever this was all about, it must have been important to him.

"Look, Varu," I took on a more agreeable tone. "I don't have the ability that you think I have. Perhaps we can try again tomorrow. Beck and Haydn will teach me to do magic, and then I'll try again."

I hoped he'd step closer so I could see his face. I waited for him to speak. I was a guest in his house and, all in all, he'd been kind to me. He'd helped make the ordeal of the last few hours a lot easier. I hated to imagine how this would have all gone down without him. I owed him. "Whatever it is that's hidden here has been safe for years. I'm sure a few more days won't matter."

"It's kept me safe from vampires and vampire hunters, but it won't keep me safe from you. Now you need it to keep you safe from vampires. You're in danger, Malka, and you need that amulet if you are to see another Christmas."

"What danger? What are you talking about?" He frightened me. So far, Varu had been agreeable and jovial, but his mood had taken a dark turn.

The breeze became increasingly fierce. It tore scraps of earth and small rocks and stones from the room's black crumbly surfaces and whipped them around the space with increasing velocity. Grains of dirt moved through the air and came to rest on my skin.

"It is not as simple as you leaving. As soon as you leave my territory, the vampires at my border will take you. You won't escape. They're waiting at the end of the street. But if that is your plan, then by all means leave."

I blinked and blinked again. Dust had settled on my eyelashes, and I didn't want it in my eyes.

Varu seemed unaffected by the swirling whirlwind of dirt and dust. "Let's go," he said. "I'll walk you out."

My mouth tasted of coppery grit. It must have worked its way through my skin, if that were possible, or up my nose. I passed through the ground, so was it possible that dirt could work its way through me? Was I about to be filled with soil and turn into a living, standing, stone fossil?

And I was fucking well, freaking out.

I couldn't breathe or talk.

For a while, I stood there with no answers.

Did Varu ask a question?

I understood Varu's concerns. I'd seen straight into his safe space. But it wasn't safe. It was hostile and trying to kill me. Was this the magic that protected Varu from invaders of his inner sanctuary?

My mouth opened to scream even though soil coated my clothes and skin, and I was being buried alive. I wasn't sure how I got there. My eyes continued blinking more rapidly. But when I opened them, I saw only darkness.

All went black before me. There was no sign of light except for flashes at the periphery, like shooting stars gone before I focused on them. I put my arms out to steady myself and feel for the wall. Grimy dirt clung to my skin and hung in the air.

Without sight, I heard the sound. Similar to a bow sliding down a violin string. That was the best description. I had no idea what made the sound or where it came from.

My hands were inexplicably, painfully hot. They weren't touching something externally hot; the heat radiated from within me.

The spinning air, the darkness, the fear, all combined to make me nauseous as if I'd been riding everything at the fairground. "Am I dying?" I tried to speak the words. My mouth moved, and air passed over the grit on my tongue. But I heard nothing but that hum. It was a god-awful sensation.

Suddenly, all the dirt started to fall away from one side of my face, but thickly caked the other. It moved swiftly like iron filings repelled from the magnet's wrong end and attracted to the other.

I blinked several times, rapidly until I didn't only register blackness. Through one eye, I saw the same room as before; however, I was no longer standing, but lying down on my stomach. My arms stretched out in front of me as if I'd been doing the butterfly stroke across the dirty floor, swimming through the soft liquid earth to get to the far end of the room. It didn't make sense. Nightmares don't. My hands no longer burned but felt warm and enclosed as if I'd slipped them under my pillow in bed.

"What happened?" I heard my anxious voice this time.

"I'm not exactly sure," Varu replied softly into my ear. He was close by, and as he spoke, he stroked my back gently. "You did magic. Can you pull your hands toward you?"

It seemed that my hands were buried in the wall. As I wiggled my fingers, the soft earth crumbled around them. In my left hand, I had hold of something. I squeezed and tried to work out what it might be.

"Did you try to kill me?" I asked Varu without pulling my hands back. If he wanted me dead, I'd already be so.

"No. But you thought I might. This is the second time I've seen you fear for your life and pull on untold resources to save yourself. It's impressive."

"You deliberately frightened me to find out how impressive I am when I'm terrified?" I couldn't put into words how much I thought that was a shitty thing to do. Right then, I just wanted to get well away from Varu, safely. I pulled my hands out of the wall and pushed myself up into a sitting position.

"Staring down death in the face provoked you into using magic. You need not impress me. My opinion of you hasn't changed one iota."

Okay, now I was curious about his opinion of me, but I would not give him the satisfaction by asking. My opinion of him, however—that had gone right downhill.

"And you found what you were searching for. It worked, didn't it?"

I looked down at my empty hands, shrugged, and then smirked. "It may have."

"Good. It's yours, and will help you survive. You should take it and start learning how to channel your powers."

I didn't know what he was talking about, but I guessed it had something to do with what I'd felt inside the earth. I thrust my hand back into the hole I'd made with my fist, or magic, or both. I wasn't entirely clear what the fuck had just happened or how my hands wound up stuck in the wall. I grasped the solid object that I'd found before and pulled it out. I had found a small box hidden in the earth.

Rather than leaning closer to take a look, Varu stood up and took a couple of steps away.

The metal of the case was barely visible under the grime. My fingers ran all over the surface as I turned it over. Sharp hinges jutted out of one side. Flakes of dirt fell away, exposing tarnished and shiny parts of a silvery surface that had been engraved with straight lines and geometric shapes or patterns. I couldn't make out much detail due to the caked-on muck and lack of light.

I held the box up, but the light from the hallway didn't fall on it. There was still light at the open door, but none of the light seemed to make it into the room. It didn't reflect off the surfaces, and it didn't cast shadows. It seemed the light didn't penetrate the invisible wall of earth that Varu could see, but I couldn't. It was most curious.

"Did the vampire in the Dracula book have a shadow?" As I asked, I realized it was an irrelevant question and apparently out of nowhere, given that there were more important things to consider. "Oh, it doesn't matter. Have you got your phone handy to give me some light over here?"

Keeping his distance, Varu obliged without comment. He shone the light on his phone in my direction.

I unhooked the feeble clasp that held the box closed. “Do you know what’s in here?”

“I do. It’s your family heirloom,” he said as I opened the lid.

That might explain his disinterested distance; he already knew what I was about to set eyes upon.

Silver jewelry lay inside the box. It was nice enough, though it didn’t appear to be anything special. Seeing it was very much an anticlimax. I poked it with my pointer finger. “Why is it hidden in here?”

“Now, I’m no expert on witches, but there is more than meets the eye in your hands. Those are powerful amulets Serina stored here for safekeeping. No witch would find it here because of the magic she’d used on this room, and no vampire, either.”

There were two small earrings in the box. I held up an earring to better examine it. It had fine silver threads woven into a pattern and looked vaguely familiar. Perhaps I’d seen my mother wearing them many years ago. I dropped it back in the box and looked at the detail on the necklace without picking it up. It contained small embedded gems of various colors, and again the same geometric pattern appeared in the detail. It jogged some memory that wouldn’t quite resurface.

Finally, I picked up the silver ring and tried it on my middle finger. It was an understated silver band and a perfect fit. “Do you mean if it fell into the wrong hands, they could use it against us?”

“Its properties are more defensive than offensive, I believe. Fire would know more. The amulets should help protect you, but I really can’t help you harness that power. At least, not any more than I already have.”

“Har, har. You call half scaring me to death like that help? You could have just shown me where to find the tin or recovered it yourself and handed it to me. It's called being civilized, you know?" God, my anger was simmering and barely under control.

"I couldn't have done any of that. I can see and move through the earth as most vampires can, and I knew the amulets were here somewhere, but where exactly was hidden from me also by magic. No vampire would have found it, and no vampire could have moved it."

I gave him my hardest stare. "What do you mean, a vampire couldn't move it? It's just jewelry." I picked up the necklace and held it out to him.

"Silver objects." Varu held up his hands and grimaced. "It doesn't kill us; a little silver merely burns; it's not pleasant. But your family heirloom is a collection of silver amulets bathed in magic. Like Fire's blades, they are all toxic to vampires."

"So witches can't find it in this room because they can't find the room, and neither can vampires. This must mean my mother planned on returning for them unless she deliberately wanted them never to resurface. Which is it, Varu?"

"Your mother wanted to keep the Selby amulets from falling into the hands of other witches. Whilst she trusted most within the Summer House Coven as it was back then, she didn't want her property to fall into the wrong hands if her enemies infiltrated her network of witches in her absence. She disbanded the coven, keeping only the most trusted people close. And she trusted me to guard this Selby treasure. Apart from her, the only people who know of its whereabouts are right here."

"She trusted Haydn with her house and money and daughter, but not with this jewelry?" I frowned. It seemed strange.

"She trusted Haydn implicitly. Nevertheless, the location of this room and the amulets were kept from him so that they were safe from other witches."

"You mean if he trusted the wrong people. Or had a break-in."

"When she placed the box here shortly before her arrest, I assumed she was coming back. I still believe that is possible. However, I have also wondered whether it was an oversight on her part, whether she'd taken account of the fact that if she and I both died, the amulets would be lost forever." Varu turned toward the door and took a few steps in its direction. "And now you have them."

"Do you think she was paranoid as part of her madness? You know, paranoia can be a symptom of mental illness."

"Serina Selby isn't mad. But she didn't confide in me so, I'm sorry, but I can't tell you who she mistrusts. You'll have to ask her."

"Bit difficult. She's incarcerated, and I haven't spoken to her for years."

"Serina isn't dead. There are many ways to communicate with her."

"Do you mean using magic?"

He nodded.

"My life's gonna change, isn't it?"

"More than you can guess," Varu answered.

I picked up a tiny stud earring, examined it, and replaced it. I then picked up the ring. "I don't suppose you can tell me anything about the magic of these. Let me guess, I need to ask Haydn."

Varu eyed it warily. "I'd suggest you put the ring back in the box, for now."

"You were the one who wanted me to find it." I sighed wearily, twisting the ring on my finger with no intention of removing it. I was fed up with all the talk of magic and being told what to do. "I need to get away and think about all this. You have a phone, Varu. Can you call me a cab? I'll go back to the hotel for the rest of the night and sleep through the morning too."

For the first time since I'd met him, sure of himself, Varu looked startled.

"No, you can't do that. Malka, you'll be safe here, in this room, or the place below where you slept earlier." He didn't say where we fucked, though that would have been the obvious reference to go for. "Whilst it is dark, significant dangers lurk beyond my territory. You mustn't leave this street. When daylight comes, it will be a little safer, but I can't be sure. You should stay with the witches and learn how to defend yourself."

Shutting the jewelry box, I got to my feet. "Excuse me while I call you out on your bullshit. You don't get to scare me into using magic twice."

"What I said earlier was true. Your enemies are gathering on the border, by which I mean, at the end of this street."

Not taking his words too seriously, I walked toward the doorway and the promise of light. "I seem to have missed something here, or you're very much confused. I don't have enemies. If vampires or anyone is gathering, they can't be coming for me. I'm nobody. And can we go back downstairs to that nice room where I can wash the dirt off my face?"

Varu shook his head but followed me out of his safe room, and I went to descend the stairs.

"There hasn't been a new earth elemental in a long time, so the Supreme High Priestess wants to meet you. She asked vampires to bring you to her, which is most unusual and is an ominous sign. You do not want to meet the council until you are in greater command of your powers. And you do not want to be unguarded with vampires. Present company excepted, of course."

I'd put out my foot to take my first step on to the stairs when Varu picked me up in his arms and held me like a baby. When I say, like a baby, I mean as if that were all I weighed. I couldn't fathom the strength involved in doing so that easily.

Before I protested and demanded to know what the fuck he thought he was doing, he pursed his lips to make a whispered shushing noise and carried me at great speed back into the safe room.

He put me down and placed a finger over his lips.

"I thought no one could hear us in here," I said.

"They can't, but I want to listen to them."

For several minutes, I heard only sounds of my own making, my breath and heartbeat, but he was listening to something. Finally, I heard something too—footsteps trudging up those stairs and two muffled voices in conversation. We watched two young people pass the open door, oblivious that we were there. The male with blue hair glanced directly at us but must have seen a wall.

"Stay here, and remember, no matter what, I am on your side, and I promised to protect you," Varu said to me as soon as the two were out of sight, and he stepped out into the light.

No matter what he said, it had been a rollercoaster of a ride with him, and I honestly wasn't sure whether to trust him or not. The only thing I knew for certain was that if he wanted me dead, I would be. I had no way to defend myself against him unless I held it in my hands. I looked at the dirt-encased box.

I'd have to enlist Haydn and Beck's help.

Out of my sight, but still within my hearing, Varu said, "Hello, Kyle. I didn't expect to meet you again so soon. How may I help you?"

CHAPTER EIGHTEEN

The invasion of a vampire's territory is often fatal
Varu Vasile

AT THE SOUND OF MY greeting, Kyle jumped and swung around. "Where did you come from?"

He looked beyond me, and I hoped Malka hadn't followed me. I couldn't hear her breathing, which was good. It meant she'd stayed in the safe room where I'd planted her.

"You two are trespassing in my house and making enough noise to wake the dead."

It wasn't the two before me that worried me—two young vampires I could handle. How many more might have come through the cemetery at the same time and be currently lurking silently in my lower basement? They may have sent these two naïve youngsters up ahead to flush out Malka with the intention of rushing up here to take her.

By sound or scent, I detected no one, but that didn't mean there weren't vampires down there. We were masters of concealment. We didn't breathe. We could be as still as stone and deadly silent. We smelt of our food and the earth, so that could be most confusing or revealing.

"Just how long have the two of you been vampires, exactly?"

"What's it to you?" Kyle grumbled. His attitude hadn't changed from earlier, which was much more surprising, given the situation he now faced.

His female companion giggled. She failed to grasp the severity of the situation.

"I'm certain you haven't been one of us for long, or you would be aware that trespassing in an elder vampire's home is a serious misdemeanor. I can kill you for this." If they were older vampires, they'd have learned to treat others with respect and to move about silently.

Some people weren't meant to be undead. Killed outright could be more merciful. In his case, Kyle should never have been turned, and he certainly shouldn't have been sent to trespass in my house.

"About a year," he answered.

I rolled my eyes, which was in keeping with the age I appeared.

"Three months," she said.

"Let's stick with three months, shall we? In vampire terms, you are a toddler. That might almost make the noise level excusable. Now, how can I help you?"

"Look, mate, we got off on the wrong foot outside. I'm sorry about that. I told you one of our cousins died in the attack in Abney Park. You saw it happen. And now, Ceyhan is also dying. After I spoke to you outside, an elder told us elemental blood might save her. We're here hoping you'll help us get some."

Kyle's words seemed heartfelt, even though they were delivered in an altogether too modern and informal way for my liking. He was only a baby in vampire years, but his lack of respect whilst trespassing on my property was vexing.

"Did you expect my help, or did you hope to sneak over my territory and into my house and grab a witch without my permission?"

It was inconceivable that two infant vampires came up with this foolhardy mission that no one in their right mind would undertake. And yet, there they were, as lambs to the slaughter trying to get the better of me in my own house. I wondered who'd sent them; whoever was behind this invasion was too wise to risk doing it for themselves.

The girl gasped. "No. We didn't intend to do anything underhand on your estate."

I couldn't be sure whether her protest was genuine or driven by fear after being caught out. Given Kyle's earlier attitude, I found it hard to believe he'd come to ask for my help, but if he had nefarious motives, he wouldn't have taken this risk, a risk that would most likely get him killed.

"I know you said you'd hand over an elemental in forty-eight hours, but that's too long to wait. We need her blood as soon as possible. Tonight. Please."

Great. I was sure Malka got all of that. I wasn't surprised. Although I wished he hadn't said it, she was bound to find out sooner or later.

"If you think I have vials of elemental blood in store, I'm sorry to disappoint. I can't help you."

The young woman's fangs descended, and her eyes widened. "What have you eaten?" she asked.

"That's a personal question from a stranger, and none of your business," I replied. "I take it you are also only recently turned?" More experienced vampires would have entered my home in silence and would immediately identify what they smelt on me.

"Three months, the same as my brother." She glanced at Kyle, and I noticed the family resemblance, which didn't stop at the two of them both having unnatural blue hair, sharp white fangs, and drool visible at the corners of their mouths. "And it's only a personal question if you fucked your food too. Is that the scent of an elemental on you? Did you drink from the girl?"

"Asya's right." Kyle nodded excitedly. A wide smile showed his fangs also fully descended and at the ready. "You didn't have that scent earlier. You smelled hungry, and that's why I thought you'd go for the bribe straight away. A bunch of delicious humans. I don't understand how you walked away like that, but you've eaten since then, and you stink like them witches."

"That smell is strong." The girl curled her tongue up over her top lip to taste the air.

I didn't wish to be reminded of the bunch of humans as I'd last seen them, cut and bloodied, presented as a feast. Too late; the image was in my head. But dealing with these two idiots in front of me was sobering. "You should detect the scent of two elementals about me, though I drank from only one of them."

"Fuck me," Kyle's eyes were wide. He could have meant it literally, he looked so aroused at the thought of the blood.

"No, thank you. I'd rather not," I replied.

"I didn't mean it in a gay way," he said. "I mean, you've been close to two elementals tonight, and I only need a few drops of blood from one of them to save Ceyhan. The most powerful one will work best. The earth girl."

"Yes. Will you help us get it?" asked the girl. "We don't need all her blood. Not much at all. We lost one cousin tonight, and we don't want to lose two."

There were so many vampires in London lately that I'd wondered where they were all coming from. This night had demonstrated there were enough vampires in East London to form a mob. And young. So many of them seemed young, as in recently turned.

We could afford a city-wide cull. From talking to Kyle and his sister, it appeared a whole British family of Turkish heritage had been turned within recent months. This alone was suspicious at a time when turning humans was strictly controlled to limit numbers. Our numbers had always been naturally limited by our food supply, along with the actions of the vampire hunters. But now the world was overpopulated with humans, and there were fewer competent vampire hunters than ever before.

Presumably, Abdil, as head of the Hackey clan, had permission to swell his tribe rapidly; however, what drove this increase in numbers? Before me, the blue-haired teenagers gave rise to a suspicion that someone, possibly Abdil himself, was creating a private army of disposable vampires to send in to do the dirty work that might get them killed.

Such missions for disposable minions might include getting dangerously close to a witch on another vampire's territory. The two Turkish girls moved ridiculously close to Fire in Abney Park. Old experienced vampires would have proceeded with a great deal more caution. And as for trespassing in a vampire's home: that was extremely dangerous and suicidal. Such acts were being done on my watch by kids from the same family. Kids who might not be aware of the formidable risks involved and who might assume immortality means invulnerability.

"I must disappoint you. I do not have access to elemental blood. I cannot help you. Now, if you leave my property promptly, we can forget that you trespassed here." I intended to sound ominous; it passed over their heads.

"But you can help us," Kyle's sister insisted. "There are elementals living along your road. We've been told by the elder that there are lots of them around here. We just have to trick one of them out onto the street."

"Easier still, you said the earth girl is staying with you," Kyle added. "Her blood will be best. It's the strongest."

I did say that did I? A slip-up—my mistake. I inadvertently enticed these intruders by hinting it would be easy to get to Malka. Witches' homes are protected by various magical charms preventing our entry. But whilst the vampires believed she was staying within a vampire's home, they thought she had little protection.

"The young lady is my guest, as I told you. You can't come in here and help yourself to her blood." I couldn't keep her in the safe room forever or the pool room that was equally well protected. "As for the other witches, their houses are all protected. We won't trick them into coming outside. We won't even be able to reach their front doors.

They're on my territory, but they have not permitted me to access any of their homes, and they do not enter mine."

"We saw a witch leave your house earlier. He had the scent of an elemental about him. It got everyone's attention," the insolent girl protested.

That would be Beck. He usually shielded his aura, but he might have let his guard down on our street, and he would have smelt of earth magic too.

Exasperated by the youngster contradicting me, my gaze wandered over her limbs and his as I assessed the best order in which to part them from their torsos.

Dismemberment was a messy business, however, and Malka was bound to disapprove. She'd probably slip on some squidgy piece of one of them and be angry about it. It surprised me to realize her disapproval mattered to me, but it did.

My primary goal was to keep Malka safe, but I realized keeping her happy and close to me were important too. I cared about Malka's opinion and her well-being.

I hadn't felt this way in years about anyone aside from Beck.

I wanted Malka's approval.

I heard a noise behind me.

Footsteps.

Breathing.

A heartbeat.

Just when I decided the blue-haired siblings might remain undead a little longer, Malka emerged, putting herself in danger.

I should have sorted this out faster and got rid of these vampires. Made sure Malka stayed safe.

CHAPTER NINETEEN

The essence of humanity
Malka Selby

I STOPPED DEAD IN MY tracks just a few feet from Varu's safe room.

Dead wasn't the right word in this context. Abrupt halt would be more apt. I came to an abrupt halt when I saw the monsters.

Their eyes were yellow, their hair blue, their skin pale and several shades of gray. Their hungry mouths hung open. My eyes fixed on their sharp canines. Kyle and his sister looked more like ravenous frightening animals than humans, in complete contrast to Varu.

He'd said something about staying in the safe room, and he'd protect me. I wished I was back there still. I should've listened to him then.

Remembering he'd also said I was powerful and the silver box in my hand would protect me, I attempted to hide my fear behind it as I took another hesitant step forward. "You sounded sincere about my blood helping your friend. How does that work?" I asked.

Varu kept his back to me but raised his hands on either side of him in a way that seemed to signal me to not come closer, or else it was to keep the monsters on the other side of him.

"Elemental blood is known to possess powerful magic in its own right. It *might* combat the poison that coated Fire's blades and is now killing the vampire he slashed in the cemetery earlier. Only might. However, it is not a certainty," Varu explained.

Already that incident had become a distant memory. It seemed like it happened days ago because so much had happened to me since then. Varu must have known all along that my blood might have been an antidote to whatever harmed the fallen vampires. At that time, I had no idea about the undead, magical silver knives, or witches.

"I really meant how do we get my blood to her? Do I have to go with you and let her feed on me?"

"That won't happen," Varu snapped.

Part of me resented being told what to do. Another part of me wanted protection from vampires as terrifying as the two in front of Varu. After all he'd said earlier, I knew why he didn't want it to happen. It might turn me on like it had Beck, and the vampire might not stop drinking in time. I might die.

Varu had made it quite clear—beware of vampires, they might kill me.

The guy, Kyle, who appeared to be in his late teens, winked and pulled out a hand full of syringes. "She doesn't need much. Just one syringe of blood should be enough."

"Then why bring more?" Varu was composed, earnest, and in command of this situation I'd just blundered into. I noticed he glanced at the stairs several times as if checking whether more vampires were on their way up.

I stepped back toward the safe room and wondered if its magic would hold strong if my enemies saw me disappear into it.

"Just in case one broke." It seemed difficult for him to speak clearly with too many big teeth in his mouth.

"I don't want anyone to die if I can save them," I said.

Without turning to speak to me, Varu answered, "You can't save everyone. And this cousin of theirs is already dead—undead." It wasn't so much that Varu had his back to me as he kept me behind him and the vampire intruders in his sight.

They snarled at him with displeasure at his lack of support.

I didn't like his callous attitude either. "They might be vampires, but if I can easily help them prevent death and suffering, then I will. It's not up to you to decide what I do with my blood any more than it is up to Haydn. Helping people is a human instinct; perhaps you don't understand it."

Inching as close as I dared to the three vampires but staying behind Varu, I held out my hand to take a syringe.

"Be careful." Varu growled. I'm not sure whether that warning was intended for the blue-haired vampires or me. "You are not exactly human."

After staring at my hand in a way that made me most uncomfortable, Kyle dropped a few into my palm.

I folded my fingers around them and snatched it back.

"Miss Earth, if you hand over your blood in that container, it might never reach the intended vampire. Your blood is too powerful to allow it to leave in the hands of vampires for persons unknown. Your blood is special."

The two blue-haired vampires bowed their heads at this.

"Then what do you suggest, Varu? How do I help?"

"You mustn't draw blood in front of vampires. If you insist on this, you will fill the receptacle in private after these children have left. And then I will deliver it to the victim of Fire's blades and ensure it goes to her and her alone."

Incredibly, the blue-haired siblings didn't argue. They showed their teeth and narrowed their eyes, but didn't speak.

"We have no time to lose, as I must make sure the witch is safe before I leave and be back here before sunrise. Where will I find Ceyhan?"

"She is in an apartment next to the Rio Cinema. If you come to the Rio, we will wait for you there," Kyle replied.

The female stared defiantly at Varu. "Can we trust you'll turn up?"

"What is your name?" Whatever expression was on his face, I have no idea, but she backed away and lowered her gaze.

"Asya," she replied. "We'll wait for you."

Under Varu's watch, Kyle and Asya slinked away, retreating down the stairs, back the way they'd come.

I stayed close behind Varu, wishing I were braver. It was starting to sink in; if he wasn't with me, I might have stepped out into the path of those two scary monsters. I wouldn't have stood a chance. And although they said they wanted me to cure their cousin, they looked as if they'd devour me.

CHAPTER TWENTY

A *short walk to safety*

Malka Selby

"DAYBREAK WILL SOON be upon us, and there is little time for me to run this errand and another I must undertake. I want to take you across the street to safety right now." The almost ever-present grin-cum-smirk had gone from Varu's features. He looked serious and concerned.

"I'll be safe in your room." I glanced back at it, just a few feet away. I actually felt safe beside Varu, and I didn't want to spend time alone in that dark, dirty shelter with a bizarre wind billowing around in it. Beck seemed at home in his water element, but I didn't feel any affinity with earth.

"You must spend the daytime with the elemental witches so they can teach you. It is twilight now; once dawn breaks, I'll not be able to take you to them."

"I'm sure I can walk across the street on my own."

"I'm sure you can, but will you get there safely? Vampires won't bother you in the daylight, but they aren't the only threat, Malka. I'd like to take you there now if I am to make this errand of compassion on your behalf."

When he put it like that, it hit me hard. He was doing a favor for me, not for the dying girl. "Don't you want to help Ceyhan, who was attacked before our very eyes?" I picked up my socks from where I'd left them, outside the door of the safe room. The fact that I began to put them back on my dirty feet was a sign that inside I was resigned to leaving this house rather than going back down to bathe and sleep. "She was struck down without any provocation. Don't you care?"

His brow wrinkled as if he didn't understand the question.

When I returned to his side, we walked up to the floor above the ground.

"I care about many things, Malka. Right now, your safety is high on that list, whereas I don't care about a vampire that I don't even know. One who trespassed on Abney Park, and by doing so and getting so close, she threatened yourself and Fire. She attacked, Fire defended."

"I don't understand why you care about my welfare but not hers. She's a vampire, like you. And she's been hurt. Whereas I'm just a girl you don't know, but you knew my mother. Those blue-haired creatures are expecting you to hand over a witch in a few days' time. That's what they said." And I thought they meant me. It was confusing because it didn't fit with Varu's behavior toward me.

We reached the hidden sliding door. Instead of pushing it open, he stopped and turned to me.

"That is only a part of it. The vampires have given me two nights to hand you over to them. They don't want you for themselves, although they might find it too hard to resist feeding on you. They intend to hand you over to the council. You must tell Haydn about this, and he will explain it to you and work out a plan for your safety. He must train you."

Varu looked into my eyes more intensely than before. There was a connection between us, which may have been there earlier, but I noticed more profoundly at that moment.

If he'd looked at the blue-haired girl earlier with a gaze as intense, I understood why she turned away.

"Malka." He looked down at the box in my hands. "Please hold the box in the same hand as the ring."

I wondered if that was a way of increasing its protective powers. As I swapped hands at his request, I asked, "Why?"

He took hold of my newly free hand. His hand wasn't cold, exactly, but not warm, either. "Because I can't hold a hand that is wearing a magical silver ring."

"Oh." My heart did a weird beat, and I blushed. I thought about my vagina getting wetter and hotter. That made me blush more as I remembered Varu would know about it.

"Before I met you, I was merely doing a favor for your ancestors by storing the amulets. Returning favors. They had done similar things to help me. However, having spent a few hours with you, things have changed. You aren't like other witches, Malka."

"I've been getting that a lot lately." My temperature was rising, and I expected my skin had gone red. He was probably talking again about me being a rare earth elemental. But with the way he looked at me, and after the evening we'd spent together, I hoped for something different. When he wasn't annoying, he made my insides buzz with desire.

"Over my long undead time, I've seen so many people die. I've become insensitive to the death of strangers who mean nothing to me. But you aren't a stranger to me. We don't know each other well yet, but I sense a close connection with you that I haven't experienced with many other people. You are special to me because of your parents and Summer House Road, but also because of who you are inside, and I want to know you better."

I may have been holding my breath with my mouth open.

His head may have been moving down slowly toward mine as he spoke.

However it happened, it just did.

His lips were on mine. His tongue in my mouth. My tongue dancing with his.

His lips tasted of something familiar and warm. I wanted more.

Inside his hot mouth tasted of... earth.

For reasons beyond explanation and that defy logic, the dry bitter flavor on my tongue with a hint of metal and rotting roots was wonderful.

I wanted him more, and more of him. We kissed with increasing passion, but he held back. Holding me back. He pulled away completely, long before I'd had my fill of him. I noticed then that he'd been keeping me at a distance at that point where the amulet box neared him. Of course, a magical silver burn would have put him off.

For a moment, I'd forgotten he was a vampire and I was a witch. And I was in danger. I was flustered. "I see what you mean about a connection," I said.

His familiar smirk was back. "Come on. There will be other nights."

God, I hope so.

He pushed open the door, and we were once again in his hallway. I brushed past to go get my new boots on; they were next to the front door where I'd left them. Glad to have an activity to focus on while I calmed down, I sorted through my confusion.

He was attractive. We'd had meaningless fun earlier. I guessed he was in love with Beck, and he was also a little bit of a sad loner. Oh, he was definitely someone I'd want to share more sexy threesomes with. It wasn't until these last few minutes together that I suspected something more attracted me to him and him to me.

He frightened me, and that might be a good or bad thing. He did it to get me to use magic, and he did it inadvertently with his strength and vampirism. He'd left me in no doubt that he could be a cold, callous, and efficient killer as a vampire, just as depicted in horror movies. And equally as sexy and seductive.

I was both attracted to him and a little intimidated by him.

He had the front door open before I'd finished getting my footwear on. We strolled out into the street together and crossed between parked cars.

There was quite a wind whistling down the street. The dawn chorus had started. Varu had said daybreak was near. I had no way to tell, and the sky looked just black to me.

"When you are ready, fill one syringe, that's all," he said when we'd reached the opposite pavement. "After that, I will watch you go up to the front door before I leave. I want to see you inside."

I pulled a syringe from my pocket. "Can you do it? I've never taken blood before."

He smiled. "What are the chances?"

"Of what?"

"Of you asking me to take your blood." His sharper teeth were visible in his smile.

"I figured you being so old, you've done most things."

"With great age comes the great experience of taking blood," he chuckled. "But rarely with anything other than my mouth." He took the syringe anyway and my outstretched arm. He appeared to know what he was doing.

"You tasted of the earth."

"So did you," he replied as he jabbed in the needle. I didn't want to watch. I looked away toward the end of the street where we'd met the lady earlier. There were several people at the end of the street, all standing still and staring at us.

"Are they friends of yours?" I asked.

Varu looked up and then laughed. "They will not believe what they've just seen. But I'll have to avoid all of them on my way to the Rio because they will all want it." He held up the tiny flask full of red blood. "I'll deliver it to the girl when you are inside, and I will make sure she and only she takes it all. Then I have another errand to run." He glanced at the top of the road at our audience of vampires. "I will be back before dawn. If I am not, if I run out of time I will take shelter, and I will be back at sunset. Now, go and knock on that door. I can't stand on the steps, as there are wards deterring vampires right there." He pointed at the bottom step.

"They'll be asleep." I climbed the brief flight of stairs leading up to the door. I couldn't detect the magic at all. The steps felt gritty under my feet, nothing out of the ordinary.

"They will be pleased you woke them. Trust me."

I knocked. The sound seemed so loud in the dead of night, but I continued to beat on the door anyway. It had to wake them, or I'd have to go back to the dark, dirt hole. I had no pleasant recollection of Varu's bedroom.

"You are safe in that house with them. You need to ask them to teach you how to use the amulets and how to shield your aura, which will make it difficult for vampires to find you. Right now, your aura is like a big, bold beacon on your head."

He didn't mean literally, but I raked my fingers through my hair anyway and then scratched my head before knocking again.

"I taste of earth, and your flavor is earth. One day we will travel and enjoy the earth together. They must train you for that."

"Okay." I had no idea what he was talking about. It might've been romantic. I decided that it was. "So just Beck and Haydn live here?" I asked and knocked again.

"And now you," he replied. "A powerful mix of fire, water, and earth. I must go." He turned and moved so fast he was a blur and then gone.

Turning my attention to the bare-chested witch standing at the open front door, I had so many questions.

CONTINUE THE STORY in book 2, Water.

1. Earth
2. Water

3. Fire
4. Air

Don't miss out!

Visit the website below and you can sign up to receive emails whenever Helen J Perry publishes a new book. There's no charge and no obligation.

https://books2read.com/r/B-A-WYYG-REXV

BOOKS 2 READ

Connecting independent readers to independent writers.

Also by Helen J Perry

Elemental Reverse Harem Quartet
Earth: Elemental Reverse Harem Quartet
Water: Elemental Reverse Harem Quartet
Fire Elemental Reverse Harem Quartet

Sons of Olympus
Defenders: Sons Of Olympus Reverse Harem Romance
Ravens: Sons of Olympus Reverse Harem Romance
Architects: Sons of Olympus Reverse Harem Romance
Sons of Olympus Trilogy Boxset

Watch for more at https://helenjperry.com/.

About the Author

Helen J Perry is a mature British mother of 3.

A bespectacled woman who loves science fiction.

A short lady, a far lady, a lover of chocolate and books in any order but together is good...

because why choose?

Read more at https://helenjperry.com/.

Milton Keynes UK
Ingram Content Group UK Ltd.
UKHW040853050124
435493UK00005B/766

9 781393 715900